WRAPPED IN RED

Thirteen Tales of Vampiric Horror

Sekhmet Press LLC

Sekhmet Press LLC

99 Rocky Fork Road
Fairview NC 28730

Copyright © 2013.

All rights reserved, including the right of reproduction in whole or in part in any form.

This book is licensed for your personal enjoyment only. This book may not be re-sold or given away to other people. If you would like to share this book with another person, please purchase an additional copy for each recipient. If you're reading this book and did not purchase it, or it was not purchased for your use only, then please purchase your own copy. Thank you for respecting the hard work of these authors.

Sekhmet Press LLC (2013)

WRAPPED IN RED: Thirteen Tales of Vampiric Horror

ISBN:978-1491026342

WRAPPED IN RED

Thirteen Tales of Vampiric Horror

If you dare...

Daddy Used to Drink Too Much . . . .*Michael G. Williams* 9

Nightbound . . . .*Patrick C. Greene* 23

Promises . . . .*Domyelle Rhyse* 49

Ye Who Enter Here, Be Damned.. . . . .. *Billie Sue Mosiman* 61

The Blood Runs Strong . . . .*Chantal Noordeloos* 71

Blood Ties. . . . .*Sarah I. Sellers* 85

Born of the Earth. . . . . *Justine Dimabayao* 95

Shattering Glass. . . . .*Brian D. Mazur* 105

The Scarlet Galleon. . . . .*Mark Parker* 119

Dangerous Dan Tucker . . . .*Maynard Blackoak* 129

Blood in the Water. . . . .*Suzi M* 141

Vermilion. . . . .*Bryan W. Alaspa* 153

My Boss is a Vampire. . . . .*Michael D. Matula* 167

Meet the Authors. 183

INTRODUCTION

by
Patrick C Greene

Before plunging our fangs into the following sanguine feasts of fiction, let us ponder the place occupied by what is perhaps nature's most human of monsters.

"What about serial killers?" you might ask, "They too can be called monsters."

True enough - but whereas a serial killer, or mass murderer if you prefer, is given the excuse of madness, vampires often retain their sensibilities. They have a need, a lust, a Crimson Calling that supersedes their logic circuits. Vampires must feed on the blood of the living to continue their existence.

Consider poor, tormented Louis, from our Queen Anne's Interview with the Vampire. Knowing he must destroy the lives of us short-timers for however long he wants to "live" he must make an agonizing decision to end a life each time he extends his own; for the blood of rats and such can only go so far.

Eventually, and in many cases immediately, the vampire makes the choice to embrace its fate; to fully become the monster, and release all of the man or woman it once was. But some traces of humanity remain, often different for each bloodsucker, that prevent it from descending to the level of a mere mindless vermin.

The stories contained herein offer a peek at vampires in various stages of acclimation to their status, from the resolutely predatory, to the fresh-born confused. We hope you'll find them entertaining - and severely discomfiting.

The vampire carries something of each of us, and so they will remain with us as long as does mortality. Find *your* point of relation within - and embrace it, as the undead embrace the darkness. Immortality is only a nibble away…

Daddy Used to Drink Too Much

Michael G. Williams

Percy came to me for the first time when Mama had been dead for sixteen days.

She'd waxed and waned like some consumptive moon for years, chasing normal life just like a cat after a string. One day in the middle of what had been a pretty good spell she said she felt real weak. That night I watched her eyes go blank while the sun set. She let out a long breath like a chain clanking and that was that. I'd never seen a person die but I could feel her go when she did.

Daddy walked over the hill to town for a preacher. When they returned the next afternoon I'd washed Mama and wrapped her in a sheet. Daddy dug the grave that night while the preacher and I sat with her. The reverend fell asleep eventually but I stayed awake all night listening to the shovel strike earth, out in the clearing beyond the creek, down a hole that could never be big enough to contain our grief.

I was sixteen so I basically ran the house already with all the time Mama spent sick. Daddy and I went through the motions for a few days without saying much, following our habits in heavy silence. Mama and Daddy grew up together in a little town over the mountains between Tennessee and North Carolina. There'd been bad blood between their people so they ran away. Mama and Daddy went southwest along the ridges, up and down old logging roads, until they found a place without any opinions about them at all.

Town was most of a day's walk on deer trails and abandoned mining or logging roads. Times were bad all over in the Depression but worse than anywhere up in Appalachia. Daddy found work for a while with a logging operation but it closed so he was stuck doing odd jobs. Mama would sew now and again. When her hands were steady she'd tat lace flowers twice as pretty as the real things. Mama would mail them to a store in Asheville; a few weeks later the store would mail her a little money after the tatting sold. Sometimes they'd send colored thread and a special request. Mama would always fret over those custom orders the most but she'd be so proud when she was done. We were all good with our hands, good at making things and doing for ourselves. I learned as much as I could from her as a little girl, before sickness crept in one bloodied handkerchief at a time until Mama was frail and tired. I read, too. Every Christmas and every birthday I'd get new shoes and books. Sometimes Mama would get books mailed to her from that store in Asheville. On warm evenings I'd sit out front under a tree and read of things that could never happen set in places far away.

Mama and Daddy were both pretty free with how I was permitted to spend my time, what I could read, how I could think. They ordered me books from all over, grownup books from distant places. Mama said they didn't want to keep me ignorant the way they'd been kept. There was one thing absolutely forbidden me: Daddy was always clear that he wouldn't have spirituous drink in the house. Sometimes he'd get worked up and rant about it. When he wasn't around once, I asked Mama why. "Daddy used to drink too much," she said. Her voice was quiet even though he was down the hill working in the corn. "He gave that up when we got together. Him and me, we saved each other from a lot of things by coming here. He's trying to save you from it, too."

I went to a school down the hollow, an hour's walk away, when Mama was doing well and they could spare me. Daddy would always ask me when I got back if there were boys at school who were "troublemakers or drunkards". He'd warn me that most young men only want one thing and they'd use liquor to get it from me. He never said what it was but I had books aplenty to tell me that.

Two weeks to the day after Mama died, Daddy stood up from breakfast and said he'd be back late that night. He went out the door and up the trail in pouring rain. I called after him to say we needed old newspapers from town--we stuffed them into the gaps in the timbers of the walls--but he didn't say anything. When Daddy got back it was nearly the next morning. He crashed into the house making so much noise I woke up thinking he was a bear. He was half-blind when he stormed into my room and he couldn't put enough words together to make sense.

I'd never seen him drunk before.

Daddy snarled like a mean dog, swung halfway around and smacked me across the jaw with the back of one big hand. I was lucky he was so drunk: he wasn't able to make a fist and he couldn't hit with all his strength.

Daddy tried to stare down at me with eyes that couldn't focus. Finally he straightened out his thick tongue enough to speak. "I'm tired of the way you keep looking like her," he said. He turned back around and walked into the front yard, right where we'd sit and I'd read. Daddy fell down and started wailing like a banshee, right there, wallowing in the mud. Eventually his sobs turned to silence and in time he took to snoring.

It was my turn to cry. I sat on the sill of my window and let the tears run down, both hands over my mouth while the trees wept raindrops around me.

The next morning I tried to move around as light as I could. At breakfast he was pale as a bucket of ashes and he kept staring at his hands. We ate in silence before he went to go do some fencing. When he got back that night I had dinner out in a pot already, with a bowl and a spoon waiting for him, and I was in my room. He skipped that to knock at my door. I didn't say anything but he came in anyway. He still looked at his hands the whole time, never at me, even when he sat down on the bed. I tried not to shy away because I thought that would probably make me mad if someone did it to me. I wanted to, though. I wanted to jump through the window and run to hide. We sat like that, waiting for something to happen, until he worked up the nerve to look me in the eye.

"I'm sorry," he said. "I sinned, and I promise never to do it again."

I nodded at him but I couldn't think of anything to say. The monster who'd torn in the night before wasn't the father I'd known. The screams he'd produced were the howls of a wounded animal. I'd never witnessed or felt things like that. He waited in silence for me to say something. Eventually he got up and went into the kitchen. I heard him ladle up some stew and sit down to eat it with big wet slurps. Words came to me at last but I was too scared to speak. My question would have to wait until morning.

"Did you ever strike *her*?" I asked it over breakfast. It was the first thing I'd said in two days. My voice sounded funny. The words tasted like metal in my mouth. I looked at him but he was looking down. He didn't say anything in return. His cheeks turned bright pink and he sagged in his chair.

I started to say I shouldn't have asked, but I didn't really think that. I'd stewed half the night. If I looked like her, and he hit me for it, had he ever hit Mama? They'd spent years being sweet in little ways, never angry. Now the whole family - our entire life together - wore a bruise to match the one on my jaw. I wanted to know, but there was more: I also wanted to hurt him. He wasn't the only one who suffered in her absence. If he had any right to be angry at the ways I was like her, I had just as much call to be angry at the ways he wasn't.

Daddy stood up and walked out, one egg still on the plate. He stopped at a crate beside the shed, pulled out a jar of something clear and trudged into the woods. When he got back that night he was able to make a fist just one time before he collapsed in the middle of the kitchen.

That night I sat on the windowsill again, perched like a little bird. I had aimed to hurt him and that fist to the face was my prize. It was a trophy. It was the closest I'd ever get to hitting back. I didn't feel pride or joy at that tiny measure of revenge but I did feel something like righteousness: the dark pride of a shameful accomplishment.

The woods were quiet. A few hoot owls greeted each other. I realized after a few minutes they'd stopped entirely. Soon I heard what had shushed them: the voice of a young man singing to himself amongst the trees. The song was one I'd heard my mother sing many times when her voice was strong:

> I'm just a wayfaring stranger
> Traveling through this world of woe
> There's no sickness, toil or danger
> In that bright land to which I go
> I'm going there to see my mother
> I'm going there no more to roam

It was a high, lilting tune and in my mind I always saw a lonesome figure tracing some far horizon as they made their way from this world to the next. The boy's voice was as pure as an angel's and I barely breathed as he neared the house. I hadn't thought on that song in years but it seemed to have been written just for me.

The singer - Percy - emerged from the woods singing one of the last lines: *I want to shout salvation's story in concert with the blood-washed band.* He looked about my age with long orange hair and pale skin gone silver in the moonlight. He wore dark clothes and an old gray cloak called an Inverness coat. It had a coal company logo on it in bright white stitching. Percy was thin, like he'd snap in a strong wind. He smiled at me. His canine teeth were bone white, sharp and long as the blades on a pair of sewing scissors.

I knew exactly what he was, from books.

Percy asked me why I was crying. I told him everything and in the blink of an eye he was next to me, his hand around my own. He whispered into my left ear, "Let's go for a walk."

We walked hand-in-hand, up and down hills and through pitch-black woods I would have feared in full daylight. He asked a hundred questions and I talked: all the words I'd fenced off in two weeks of silence since Mama died. I told him more than that, too: things I'd never thought to say to another person. He listened like it was important to him. Hours later I realized he had led me in zigzags back at the cabin, right to my window, without me even noticing.

"Will he drink again tomorrow?"

"I don't know," I said.

"I'll be here." Percy's eyes were half-closed, very dark and twice as sharp. He leaned in close to whisper. "I'll tell him he has to stop." It made me feel better than I could've hoped.

I'd never kissed a boy before and didn't know what to expect but I knew it was about to happen. Percy clamped his mouth against my neck instead, where the big veins are, and bit down with those perfect white teeth. Compared to the bruises on my jaw and around my eye it barely hurt at all.

The next morning I went out to do some chores so Daddy could be alone when he woke up. Around mid-day he ate a little bread and plunged his head straight into the creek out back before hefting his toolbox and going to do some work. I didn't see him at supper. He walked in just before the clock struck ten that night while I sat at the table.

Daddy sagged in the chair across from me, his skin a waxy gray. He drew a breath but this time it was my turn not to let him talk.

"You said you wouldn't do that again."

"I'm sorry." His voice was clotted.

"Never again." I tried to meet his eyes but he avoided me. It didn't matter. I was sure of myself and he sounded like he was a hundred miles away. I had the advantage.

"I promise."

"I've got someone around to make sure you keep that promise." I nodded at a window. "Out there, in the woods. My friend Percy's going to stop you."

Percy had told me he'd wait for Daddy to return, and he had. We had waited hours for this. Percy was standing in the window, right outside.

Daddy went pink and purple-red in about two seconds and stood away from the table. "Who the hell is that? Is that some boy from school?" He was instantly furious: ashamed of himself and of having someone know his shame. Daddy's voice shook as he bellowed. "Get in here, boy!"

There was a sound like a scythe through grass and Percy was standing inside with us. He'd gone around the house, through the door and across the kitchen in less time than a heart takes to beat. He was scrawny next to Daddy but he was ten times as strong. Daddy balled up one fist but Percy put his own tiny hand around that fist and twisted it hard. He hissed like a big cat and swung so fast I barely saw his other hand connect with Daddy's jaw. Daddy flew backwards and slid rhythmically across the old slat floor. Percy leapt through the air before he'd stopped and landed astride him. He dragged Daddy halfway to sitting by the back of his neck and punched him square in the face once; twice; a third time. Percy's features twisted in rage and he roared once, echoing across the little cabin, then he leaned close. His voice was real quiet and smooth. He wasn't breathing hard at all. "You don't tell me what to do," he whispered. Daddy's eyes went real wide and shook. Percy's put a hand over Daddy's mouth to keep him quiet. "You be real sweet to her. Be a good boy and do what I say, or else. You got that?" Percy's fangs clicked his other teeth as he spoke, right in Daddy's ear. It twisted my guts--more fists, more anger--but it was also enticing in a way I wouldn't have expected. Close together like that, they made the same mockery of intimacy that Daddy had when he slapped my face with hands that had previously worked to provide.

Daddy gawped at Percy's ultimatum but finally nodded.

"Good," Percy said. "Now clean up while we go for a walk."

Tears sprang into the corner of Daddy's eyes. Percy let him go and he looked at me with the very last of the anger he'd felt when he saw Percy at the window. "My daughter, taking off into the woods with the Devil?"

"Better the woods with the Devil than this house with you." I ran one hand down my own cheek after I spoke.

That night Percy sang me songs from all over while we walked.

The next day Daddy was real nice, and the day after that, and we went on that way for three weeks. Daddy acted right, I didn't get hit and Percy would show up after sunset to sing me songs while the moon got thin, disappeared and came back.

On our last walk together, Percy sang to me at first but soon we fell silent. We had a route we walked together, a swooping whorl threading down deer paths between ambitious sweetgum saplings. He hadn't needed to guide me down for a while but I let him anyway because we both enjoyed playing gentleman and lady. We came back to the house and he lifted me into the window but stopped after and looked right into my eyes. His were green and bright like new moss, alive and alert and shining like the sun.

"I need to ask you something," he said.

I knew what was coming. I said, "It's late. Ask me tomorrow."

"No, I need to ask now, with the moonlight on you just like this." He licked his chapped lips and pushed out all the words at once. "Won't you let me turn you? Be with me forever, just like this, just like you are now. We'll go away." His eyes shuddered a little as he looked away from me, towards some future he could see across dark hills. "There's nothing here for either of us, so why waste time? You could get sick and die, or have an accident or your daddy could go off again. If you let me, you'll be safe and strong. There won't be anything could hurt you." His beautiful green eyes pleaded with me to say yes, to show him my throat, to submit.

That future he saw was invisible to me. "No," I whispered. I leaned in and rested my right ear against his silent chest, slipping both hands around his narrow waist. "I don't want that. I love you like crazy, like I don't know how to say. Every day I work just so I can be in my window as soon as it's dark: so I can hear it when you sing to me across the woods." I swallowed hard. "But I don't want to be what you are. I don't want to be like this forever. I want to grow up and live and die old. My mama didn't get to do that."

"You don't have to live her life just because she can't."

I loved him for saying that, but I leaned back and shook my head. "I know," I smiled. "But I want to stay me." I put a hand on his chest. "You have to go now. Kiss me goodnight." He did, and I thanked him before I shut the window and closed the curtain.

I didn't sleep. I lay there and thought about why I'd told him no: that moment when he'd run in and stood over Daddy with his fangs out. The more I'd thought about that, the more I'd realized one thing: he'd done to Daddy just like Daddy did to me. Maybe Daddy deserved it. I didn't deny enjoying it, either. Still, I couldn't get that out of my head, when Percy stood over Daddy and roared just like Daddy'd done to me. I thought of what I'd asked, what had gotten me hit the second time: had Daddy ever struck Mama that way? I felt I knew the answer now, and when I saw Percy's lace-fine fists beat Daddy in the face it was the same story all over again. He was young and angry and he'd stick up for me, sure, but if we ran off I'd be the only one around the next time he flew into a rage.

Percy was right: I didn't have to live Mama's life.

For three days, everything was normal. Daddy didn't speak unless spoken to and I kept the house going. Every night I'd lay in bed wondering if Percy would really stay away. I had started to think he would, that maybe I should patch things back up with Daddy since he was acting right.

Percy came back the fourth night, right after the sun went down.

The front door flew apart like a bomb had gone off and Percy was standing where it had been. He stepped inside. Daddy was sitting at the table reading an old Bible. Before he could do anything, Percy knocked it out of Daddy's hands and sank his fangs into Daddy's neck. Daddy screamed until those teeth tore out his throat. Blood sprayed in a bright red arc in front of them. Percy's jaw dropped open like a snake's and he wrapped his lips all the way around the hole in Daddy's neck. He pushed Daddy up against the wall, and held him there. Daddy went white real quick as Percy made these deep, thick, gulping sounds. I heard a snap and realized Percy was crushing Daddy's rib cage.

I screamed as loud as I could but Percy didn't stop.

Daddy went whiter than white--whiter than Percy— before sliding down the wall and onto the floor like a rag doll. Percy squatted and grabbed each of Daddy's legs, squeezing them in his hands like he was kneading dough. I could hear the bones splinter. Daddy's eyes were open fading, just the way I'd seen Mama's do when she died. He wasn't moving or screaming or anything. He just lay there while Percy wrecked both his legs in less time than it takes to say that aloud.

Percy looked at me, blood all over his face. "I can't make you go with me," he said, "But I can make him suffer. This is the price he has to pay for hurting you: he'll be at your mercy forever." He'd said I'd forever be the way I was right then if he turned me. I opened my mouth to speak but I was too slow. Percy bit into the ghostly flesh of his own wrist. Thick, black blood like old engine oil welled up. He shoved it against Daddy's frozen mouth. "You think a drink will make you strong? Have a drink of this."

At first, Daddy just lay there and the blood ran into his mouth but after a few seconds he latched on so hard Percy flinched. I wondered if Percy had ever done this before: turned one of us. He let Daddy drink for a few seconds before shoving Daddy back again. Percy ran his own tongue over the wound and wiped his mouth on the sleeve of that Inverness coat. All it did was get blood everywhere.

Our eyes met in silence for a second, then Percy walked back out the door. I saw him step into the woods, into the darkness, I feared I'd never see him again.

It was another night for crying. Daddy lay in the middle of the floor and wept to himself, his hands to his face. When it was just headed towards daylight I crouched down in front of him and cleared my throat.

Daddy wouldn't look at me, but he did flinch when he realized I was right there in front of him. I reached out and put my hands on his, pulling them away from his face.

Great big tears of blood had dried on his cheeks.

"I've been working on getting your room ready," I said. "We need to get you in there before the sun comes up. Percy told me he has to stay out of the sun so I hung up some quilts over your window."

"It's a curse from God," Daddy wasn't looking at me and he wasn't really talking to me. "It's a curse for the things I did to you and to your Mama and all the other little sins of my life. It's a curse for being proud and thinking I could beat the Devil. It's a curse for taking to drink."

"Hush. It's just another problem to solve." I wasn't kind when I said it. I put my hands under his armpits and tried to stand, to hoist him up, but he was dead weight. "Come on, you have to help." Under all the shock and anger and sadness--all the ways I realized were just another roll in some player piano striking the same few notes for our family time and time again--I was surprised to realize I was also annoyed. Petty and threadbare as that emotion seemed at the time, I felt tired of having to wash the same emotional bowl. Everything had been okay when Mama was here but now it was just one stupid situation after another and they were all the same one over again from different angles.

Daddy wasn't helping. "Leave me here," he croaked. "Let me see Godly light one time." He blinked some of the fog from his eyes. "Kill me, girl. Kill me right now before I hurt a living thing."

With great frustration I let go and stood up. "Don't be stupid," I said. "You don't want that."

"Don't tell me what I want!" His voice was like the ghost of being drunk again. His voice faltered and he got quiet. "Don't tell me what I want."

"Fine," I snapped, "But we have to get you in that bedroom."

"Why?" He looked directly at me and I blinked at the sudden shock of seeing that much pain in a person's eyes. When Mama had died we'd both walked around empty for a while. Now, sitting there, Daddy didn't have that empty, passive suffering of someone who's waiting for life to regain its color. His suffering was impassioned and alive.

"Because he wants me to," I said. I startled myself with the realization even as I said it. "That's why he did this: he can tell himself he did it to punish you but he just wants to make sure I suffer without him. I'm not giving him the satisfaction. I'm not letting him smother to death everything I've got in this world so I'll have nothing to stop me running off with him." I pointed out the door, the way he'd gone, as though he were standing in the trees watching us work it all out.

Perhaps he was.

My mouth felt dry, but I kept going. "It isn't all about him, though. It's also about you, and about me. Mama said you saved each other. You were a drunk but she loved you enough to take off across the hills and give up everything else in her life. I want to know why. You could hit me a hundred times, maybe, and even though I wouldn't forgive you for that it would still be true that Mama saw something good in you. She saw in you the Daddy I had while she was still alive and she saw him before he existed. I think that's still in you. I want to find it and I won't have a chance to do that if you die now."

We stared at each other in silence.

"Now drag yourself to bed, Daddy, because the sun's about to come up." I looked meaningfully at the door and at his room before shutting myself away inside my own.

I didn't sleep when I got between the covers. I listened instead: for the birds that sing at sunrise and for Daddy to drag himself across the floor. I heard him flop around some and scrape his boots across the wooden slats. He was moving arm-over-arm, falling heavily forward every time he took another "step" on his elbows. I was sure it hurt.

I listened to Daddy inch forward with agonizing grunts and groans until finally I heard him fall into the mud again, outdoors, beyond that busted front door. I waited for him to cry out, to ask me to help him get back inside, but he didn't say a word. The sun started to come up and I went to stand at the door out of my room just in case he called to me, but still nothing. I didn't want him to die, but if we were going to do this we had to do this together.

I could see him out there, flat on his belly in the dirt, long streaks of brown blood behind him. Daddy stood up and stared up at the blue-black sky and watched the sun climb over the ridge. When its rays burst across the yard, Daddy shrieked just once. If he tried to say anything, he didn't get the chance. He was instantly a pile of smoking ash, a grotesque and crumbling statue of himself with his arms outstretched. He'd burned up in the blink of an eye. I thought of Lot's wife: turned to a pillar of salt when she gazed back in longing at the place where she'd lived a life of sin.

I'd told him I wanted to see the part of him that made my Mama run away, and he'd shown it to me: the capacity to imagine a life without constant anguish, a life that would let the two of them be free of the terrible things their families and they had done before. Now, with his final act, he'd shown me the same mercy. He had chosen to put an end to what would have been an awful life for both of us.

I thanked him many times that morning while I cleaned up the mess and I haven't stopped thanking him yet.

***

Nightbound

Patrick C. Greene

Freedom should be better than this, Blake Zagarino thought, dabbing sweat from his neck with a bandana, as yet another bout of shrill laughter assaulted his ears from the backseat of the lot-fresh, stolen Buick. But Zagarino played it cool.

DeWitt, the laughing man, raised a snub-nosed .38, childishly making shooting sounds while he mimicked the gun's recoil. Like the .38, he was small, oily and deadly.

"*Blamblamblam!*" DeWitt bellowed, "No! Don't kill me!" he said in a mocking falsetto, then came a fit of giggly laughter, and finally: "Please! I got a daughter!" More laughter. "*Blamblam!* Daddy's gonna be REAL late tonight, sweetheart! *HeeheeheeHEEEE!*"

Continuing to drive the winding road between hilltop homes, Zagarino did nothing to betray the disgust he felt with his partner, confident DeWitt would grow distracted soon, as he usually did. Bonner, the boss of their criminal triumvirate, was considerably less patient. "Put that down, you idiot!" he snarled. "If you get us caught, I swear I'll beat you *dead*, boy!"

Bonner's grayish brush cut glistened with sweat, which then rolled down into his stubble. Zagarino hoped he wouldn't turn his head around too swiftly and thus sling some of the grimy sweat onto him.

"Okay okay, sorry" DeWitt began, "I can't help it! Man was that fun! I never knocked over no armored car before! And wasted the guards to boot! WHOOO!"

"Shaddup," Bonner ordered, and DeWitt looked out the window, issuing a low titter to himself.

"If your girl's info was right, we've got at least ten minutes before the guards are supposed to check in. We should be dug in by…" Zagarino checked his watch and calculated. "…11:30."

"Don't you worry about MaryAnn. She wouldn't tell me wrong. She knows better. You just better be right about this hideout," Bonner grumbled.

"Couple that owns it live in Eastern Europe," Zagarino reiterated again, "They only come here on vacation. And who'd wanna vacation in this Godforsaken heat?"

"Get used to it, Zag. Two weeks, we'll be in Mexico."

"Now you're talkin' *my* language!" DeWitt enjoined. "Here I c-c-c-come, senoritas!"

"Gotta eighty-six this car," said Bonner. "Hope you boys are up for a hike."

Zagarino drove into one of the many small forests surrounding and separating the clusters of secluded and exclusive neighborhoods in the rural outskirts of Chicago. He drove behind a thick pine and they quickly concealed the Buick under branches and lightweight fallen pine logs, until it looked something like a teepee fort made by local kids or hobos. The forest ended at a weedy hill some sixty yards high and steep enough to be daunting to outsiders; one of the selling points pushed by its developers and realtors.

There was no wind to cool the cons, who had grown used to the cool comfort of medium security. Trudging up the uneven, scrubby hill carrying four heavily-loaded canvas sacks, Zagarino wished he had exercised more in prison. But he had never cared for the company of the aggressive, steroid-addicted meatheads who hovered around the weight benches and the penitentiary's depressing excuse for a running track.

DeWitt shared his regret. "Hey, slow down!" he huffed. He had stopped entirely-and this would not be acceptable to Bonner. Though stocky and physically very tough, Bonner was in his early fifties and heading toward "pudgy" himself, but he wasn't about to abide DeWitt's complaints.

"DeWitt, get your ass up and move it! Now!"

"Wait a minute, boss. ...I need a break. Heat's killing me...all this cash must weigh a hundred tons."

"Get up, or so help me, dipshit, your corpse will fry in this heat," Bonner warned.

"Okay, okay. How much further, Zag?" DeWitt asked, as much to buy another second of rest as to know.

"The house is just a few yards from the top of the hill," Zagarino answered evenly, and started moving.

From the top of the hill, there was still a good ten yards to the large, oddly plain house. The nearest neighboring homes were a good distance away and arranged so that rows of trees fairly concealed them from one another; the very wealthy apparently needed comfortable degrees of separation even from one another. But the three desperate men nonetheless hunkered low, using the high weeds of the unkempt backyard to hide behind as they dragged the moneybags around to a front door sheltered under a pair of leafy poplars.

Drawing a small black case from his pocket, Zagarino kneeled and went to work on the lock with measured finesse, feeling the antsy tension coming off his partners in stinking waves.

"Come on, man!" DeWitt stage whispered.

"Shut it," Bonner ordered quietly, knowing that the kind of work Zagarino did was best not rushed.

After a moment, Zagarino removed his tools from the lock and rolled them up in their pouch, then stood, opened the door and took a step inside, into pure darkness.

DeWitt tried to go in next, but Bonner muscled him aside, raising the sturdy flashlight he had taken off one of the dead guards. He traced its beam over the sheeted furnishings, capturing huge dust motes that seemed to swim toward them curiously. For a long moment, they silently took measure of the enormous front room, the dusty stairway that dominated the center, the many doors on either side leading to reading rooms and the like. Swinging double doors at the rear gave way to a kitchen, beside which was a plain and heavy black door that could only lead to a basement.

"Made in the shade, man!" DeWitt said aloud.

Bonner turned to him sharply. A mouse scurried somewhere close to the walls, drawing startled grunts from DeWitt and him.

"It's all right," Zagarino reassured them, "Just vermin. No one's been here in months."

Bonner dropped the money bags on the floor, and the other two followed suit. The muffled thump echoed back at them from the mahogany walls.

"These curtains are thick as a woolly mastodon's hide," noted DeWitt.

"I don't even care what that is," Bonner grumbled. "Open 'em, but just a little bit, so we can see to move around in here,".

Bonner wiped sweat from his brow as he regarded the dark forms of his partners. "MaryAnn'll be here after five."

Zagarino cleared his throat, sparking a zippo to light a three-pronged silver candelabra. "About that..."

"...What?" Bonner asked sharply.

"You sure we can trust her? I mean, she is selling out the company she works for. Who's to say she wouldn't do the same to us?"

Bonner laughed. "That bitch wants money, Zagarino. Just like all of 'em. When I was in the joint, and she was sending me those letters, I knew right away that what she really wanted was a man that could give her a great big, thick…wad of dough. And that's all." Bonner's face took on a discomforting, slimy grin, as he grasped his crotch. "Fine by me, 'cause she's damn sure gonna give me my money's worth before it's all over. And if for one minute, I start thinkin' she's lookin' to screw me in anything less than the literal sense... BAM!...just like I'd do to either one a you. Got it?" Bonner's face looked as crazy as it was cruel in the crossfire of candlelight and muted sunshine.

"Yeah," Zagarino intoned dispassionately, "Got it."

Bonner turned to DeWitt. "What about you, Dimwit?"

"Got it. And it's…ya know, *Deee*-Witt."

"Good." Bonner ignored the correction. "Now before everybody starts moving around, exploring our new digs, let's all sit down and count the take."

Zagarino took the candelabra into a small open dining room just off the hallway. "This looks about right," he advised. They took the bags in and hoisted them onto an antique table that looked to have been restored several times; and was probably no less than a hundred years old.

It was understood that Bonner would be the one to dump the wrapped bundles. "I played a lot of poker, boys," he said. "Don't try to slip something by." A couple of the bundles slid from the top of the first pile onto the floor.

"Pick it up, DeWitt," ordered Bonner, as he checked Zagarino's face, his hand hovering near the .45 tucked in his waistband.

DeWitt picked up the bundles, taking a moment to inspect them with reverent wonder, then smiled at Bonner as he tossed them onto the others. Bonner sat, satisfied that his partners were smart enough to stay on the right page.

DeWitt sighed as though his mind had been taxed to the limit as he finished the last bundle and placed it on top of the mountainous stack. "That's another ten grand."

Zagarino meticulously straightened this bundle as he had all the others, making a geometric wonder of the paper pyramid. "That brings us to 840,000 dollars."

"Not bad," Bonner assessed with a thoughtful rub of his crew cut, "but I was hoping for a cool mil. All right then. Let's bag it back up."

"Hold on!" said DeWitt, "I wanna look at it a while."

Bonner sighed. "You can look at it later. Now bag it like I said, bitch." He pointed toward the black door. "And get it into the basement."

DeWitt did not hide his disappointment, as he began tossing the bundles back into the sacks, issuing a breathy "Shit..."

Zagarino smiled to himself, not bothered at all to see his feat of engineering unceremoniously disassembled. "I'll find more candles."

DeWitt, finally losing his adrenaline rush and crashing toward exhaustion, struggled to drag the rug - onto which he had piled the money bags to save trips - down the open basement stairs, grumbling to himself all the way. It wasn't until he arrived at the bottom and stood to straighten his back that he realized the only light reaching the dank, cavernous subterranean room was a tiny shaft of daylight that filtered from the window upstairs.

DeWitt shivered in the dankness, feeling a sudden disconcerting chill. He opened his eyes wide to make them adjust. Old furniture, antiques, and other hunched skulking forms began to take shape.

DeWitt had seen enough; he ran up the stairs, fighting off another shivering spell.

Zagarino stood to the side of the living room's bay window and peeked through the small gap DeWitt had opened, at a well-used 2001 Firebird slowly wheeling past. The rag top was down, no doubt so its driver, MaryAnn

Kleiber, could set up wolf whistles, sonic shadows of flattery that followed her everywhere but here.

Zagarino opened the shade slightly wider and waved, calling to Bonner. "Looks like your lady-friend's here, Bonner." MaryAnn spotted him and sped toward the driveway.

"It's about fucking time," Bonner groused. Zagarino watched as he swaggered to the door, crudely grabbing his crotch in anticipation. Zagarino followed him, mostly out of curiosity as to how the reunion would play out.

Before she even knocked, Bonner opened the door and tugged her inside roughly by the arm.

"Oh!" MaryAnn exclaimed, then took on a nervous smile. "Hi Vic! Glad to see you too!"

Bonner ignored her small talk, looking her over from head to toe with unconcealed lust. There wasn't much concealed about MaryAnn either--very short cut-offs and a babydoll T-shirt that said "Dish" in a playful, sparkly font. She was a little old for such attire, but still young enough that only women would make that observation. And Zagarino, of course.

Bonner closed the door, while Zagarino, like a gentleman, took the box of supplies she held.

"I brought food, some candles and a flashli-" Bonner cut her off, grabbing her roughly and kissing her like a man who hadn't been with a woman in ten-to-twenty--cut short by six, of course, figuring in the escape. She played along quite convincingly for a good while, then opened her eyes. Perhaps creeped out by Zagarino's stoic observation of their mating ritual, she pulled away. "Whoa..! Lemme breathe, big man!"

"You can breathe when you're dead," he said.

"Wait!" MaryAnn cast a quick, doubtful glance at Zagarino. "I heard on the radio that...the guards were...shot."

"So?" Bonner shrugged, "That a problem for you?"

"Uh…No, not really…I just got a little nervous, that's all."

"We're better off. Nobody to I.D. us now," Bonner explained. Zagarino smiled thinly in agreement.

"Sure, of course, Vic…Um…what about the cash?" she ventured.

"We got enough."

"…Can I see it?" She was testing her boundaries. And her luck.

"Later," was all the response Bonner bothered with, before he took her by the wrist and pulled her toward the stairway.

DeWitt entered, ready to relax from the long day's exhilarating events. But upon seeing MaryAnn, he immediately perked up. "Damn!" he gushed.

Not waiting to see Bonner blow his fuse, Zagarino interjected. "Why don't you introduce us, Bonner?"

The disarm worked. "MaryAnn, this is the boys. Zagarino, DeWitt."

DeWitt extended his grubby hand. "Nice to meet ya! Got any friends, or… sisters or anything?"

Maryann laughed uncomfortably.

"Is your mom single?" DeWitt continued.

"Shut up, DeWitt. We'll be upstairs for a while, boys. No interruptions." Bonner raised his .45 to underscore his next point. "No cute ideas. Right?"

Upon affirmatives from DeWitt and Zagarino, Bonner grabbed MaryAnn's wrist again. "Come on, baby."

"Wait, Vic," MaryAnn ventured, "Can I please see the money?"

Bonner had very little left of what passed for patience or decorum in his world. "I told ya, it's in the basement, safe and cozy. Now come on."

Bonner started to drag her up the stairs again, when DeWitt stopped him. "Hey Vic?"

Bonner turned to DeWitt slowly, sighing with building frustration. DeWitt huddled close to whisper "Is it okay if I watch?"

Bonner closed his eyes tightly for a long time, as if trying to conceptualize DeWitt's request. "…What..?"

"I'll just sit there and be quiet. That okay?"

Bonner pie-faced DeWitt, pushing him to the floor. "No you can't *watch*, you freaking pervert! What the hell is wrong with you?"

"Nothing boss. I just...it's been so long..."

Bonner loomed over DeWitt, pointing at him with a stubby sausage-like finger. "Listen, you fucking retard. If I hear one little peep outside that bedroom door, I will stomp you into a puddle of jelly. You got that?"

"Yeah, yeah."

"Come on," Bonner huffed, storming up the stairs with MaryAnn in tow.

DeWitt waited till he was gone to stand up. "Shit. I was just asking. He didn't have to be an asshole about it."

"Don't let it bother you." Zagarino offered a brotherly pat on the shoulder, holding it despite his distaste for the sweaty dampness he felt there. "Why don't you go down in the basement for a little while? It's cool down there. Smell the money, walk around a little. Zagarino handed him a flashlight. "Here."

"I dunno. Bonner said-"

Zagarino cut him off with a chuckle. "You really think he's going to bother to check on what we're doing down here for the next little while?"

DeWitt thought a moment. "Yeah, you're right. Good idea. I'll do it. It's cool down there." And DeWitt shuffled away, sighing his lingering disappointment at losing a chance to watch sex.

Standing behind the naked MaryAnn, Bonner shoved her, face-forward, toward the bed where she caught herself with her hands. Now bent over, MaryAnn received a stinging smack on the ass. "Ow!" she squealed.

"Ya like that, dontcha?" Bonner said.

"Oh yes, Vic," MaryAnn said less-than-convincingly, "I like that."

Bonner didn't really care, but he did like the way the candlelight played on her curves; soft but smooth the way he liked his women. And the real thing was a damn sight better by far than worn contraband nudie photos. Bonner spun her over and threw her on the bed, grinning at her like a devil mask as he let her perfection cast its spell on his mind and groin.

MaryAnn was not frightened; her smile was a mask too, a cupie-doll's plastic devotion to a carny mark.

Bonner whipped his belt off through his waistband smoothly and tossed it away, his eagerness pushing at his zipper.

DeWitt descended the basement stairs, too hurt by the embarrassing treatment Bonner had given him to remember that he had been spooked being down here before. He stopped at the bottom to take a breath of the cool air and muttered to himself, "Grouchy fuck. I'da let *him* watch."

He clicked on the flashlight and went to the money bags. After peeking up the stairs, he reached in and took a bundle, sniffing it with pleasure. "Yeah, that's the shit. They oughta bottle this smell."

But remembering Bonner's threats, he quickly grew tense, despite Zagarino's reassurance.

Zagarino.

Something about the bespectacled former embezzler – the so-called brains of their outfit- always seemed a little off to DeWitt. He looked up the stairs again and returned the bundle of cash to the bag.

Enjoying the feel of the cool air on his sweaty face, DeWitt looked around at the sparse collection of junk that littered the basement in various clusters in some form of organization known only to the vacationing residents. He came to a large, dusty portrait leaning against the wall atop a plastic-sheeted Victrola. Blowing away the layer of filth, he made out an oil painting of a regal-looking couple in their thirties; a tall blonde man, a buxom brunette at his side.

"You must be the master of the house," DeWitt whispered sardonically to the rendered man. Then his gaze fell on the woman, and he smiled, rubbing his finger down beautifully-detailed lips to the textured image of her breasts. "Yeah. Now you look like a hot little thing."

Losing interest, he shuffled along. Across the room, in the darkest corner, he spotted something that interested him very much; two deep oblong boxes lying side by side. He went to them and scanned the flashlight beam over them, finding only plain, unfinished hardwood. Locating the crack between lid and frame on the nearest, he tucked the flashlight under his arm and carefully lifted the lid-but saw only a vague black form within. DeWitt leaned forward, turning his flashlight beam onto the shape.

It was a well-dressed man in his thirties - clearly the model for the gentleman in the portrait. DeWitt gasped with fright and scrambled backwards, dropping the flashlight as he fell.

Breathing heavily, he stared at the open coffin that seemed to grow and shrink in the shadows with the damaged flashlight's odd lopsided rolling and flickering. Trying to catch his breath, he stood, careful not to make a sound.

Picking up the light, he kept his eyes on the box. He smacked the flashlight, making it brighten for a moment, and took slow steps toward the box. Looking in, he saw that the figure had not moved. He drew the .38 from his waistband. "H...Hey!"

He poked the figure with the gun barrel--no movement. He poked again, harder, then held a hand over the figure's mouth and nose, and felt nothing. He checked for a pulse, as well as he knew how.

"Deader'n shit," he whispered to himself. Scanning down the corpse's gaunt frame, he came to on an exquisite topaz-jeweled gold ring on the decedent's hand that glittered in the light's beam. "Oh shit!" he exclaimed.

He tucked his gun under in his waistband, placed the flashlight on the corpse's chest, and gingerly lifted the stiff hand to pry the ring off. With some effort, he finally worked it free. He held it up, chuckling, admiring its gleam in the flashlight beam. "Thanks pal," With a grin, he said to the body, "I'll take real good care of it!"

Realization dawning on his face, he looked back at the portrait. "...Hey! That's gotta mean..."

He turned to the second box with a wild look, then back to the portrait, and finally back to the male cadaver. "That your little lady-friend over there, pal? Huh?"

DeWitt grinned wider, as he dropped the lid on the dead man. He went to the second box.

Opening it, he issued a triumphant laugh, then a disgusting snicker, as he illuminated the beautiful woman at rest therein. "Jackpot. Well preserved, aintcha sugar?"

Turning his head sideways licentious-wistfully, DeWitt rubbed her cheek, stroked her neck. Finding an elegant pearl necklace there, he snapped it off and dropped it in his pocket, still leering at the corpse. He slowly touched her breast with excited, shaking fingers, then began to loosen the front of her blouse, exposing cleavage. His heart thumped and his erection grew, like a teen boy seeing his first picture of a naked woman.

Finally he had pulled the woman's blouse apart, exposing both pale breasts. He was hardly able to believe his good fortune. He leaned in to kiss her...

"DeWitt," said a soft voice behind him.

Gasping with fright, DeWitt leapt up and spun, his gun ready.

"Whoa! Easy!" Zagarino said.

"Shit! You scared the hell outta me!" DeWitt nearly coughed.

"What are you doing down here?" Zagarino asked.

"Just... looking in these fucking boxes, that's all." DeWitt said, his words stumbling over each other.

"Oh yeah? What's in 'em?"

"Nothing!...nothing," DeWitt said too quickly. "Just old junk."

"Hm. Well…come on up. I need your help. It's getting dark. We need to light some more candles."

"Oh sure, yeah!"

After Zagarino trudged back up the stairs, DeWitt reopened the box and spared a last lustful look at the dead beauty, then let the lid drop, and left.

Bonner sat at the edge of the bed in his prison issue underwear, checking the magazine of his pistol by the candlelight. Behind him, the pensive Maryann pulled on her panties. "That was real nice, Vic."

Bonner laughed cynically. "Sure, baby."

She thought to perk her breasts out a bit before asking "Um…do you think I could have a little advance on the cash?"

Bonner glowered at her suspiciously. "For what?"

"I'd just...feel better if I could hold it, you know."

"Riiiight." Bonner chuckled. "Don't you trust me?"

"Of course I do, Vic. It's not that."

Bonner stood, ignoring her display of breasts, grabbing her arm and pulling her toward him, till they were eye to eye. "Well let me tell you something. I damn sure don't trust you. So you can just wait till we get to Mexico. Then you'll get your cut and you can go do whatever the hell you want. Come back here, for all I care. Till then, you stay right here by my side and do what I say." He pulled her to her knees roughly. "*Everything*…I say. Got it?"

"Okay Vic. Sure!" she said breathlessly, looking up at him with doe eyes.

"Good. Now let's get down there before DeWitt screws something up."

Timidly standing, in case that wasn't what he wanted, she said" I…I need…to freshen up a little, Vic."

Bonner grimaced at her a moment. "Whatever." He left with a slam of the door.

Maryann stood before the dusty mirror on the dresser next to the door. She took a brush from her purse, and regarded her reflection, troubled. "Oh Maryann. What the hell are you doing?"

She began brushing her hair, not hearing the closet door opening slowly behind her, not seeing its movement reflected behind her beyond the tiny candle's boundaries of illumination. Though looking at her reflection, MaryAnn only saw a montage from a life of doing things in what seemed to be the easy way. "Remember when there was more to you?"

Maryann stopped brushing, for a moment, sensing something...*off*. But regret bade release, attention. "This is the last time, little girl," she swore, pointing the brush at her reflection. "Then, you get a nice guy- a car salesman. Or a politician."

She resumed brushing, unable to see the tall figure that cast no reflection, gliding with unholy silence to stand behind her, close enough to take in the scent of her neck.

Then she shivered.

"This place gives me the heebie-jeebies."

She felt an icy hand clamp over her mouth - but in the mirror, she saw only her lower face being contorted unattractively. She dropped the brush, her scream meeting only cold flesh, as she felt a strong man pulling her close from behind - though the mirror showed her nothing.

She felt a cold wetness on her neck, like someone licking her after drinking ice water - then felt the breathtaking pain of steel-hard fingers plunging into her back, and exiting her chest. Now there was something to see - a hand that seemed to be made of blood displayed her heart in the mirror. She felt cold lips sharp fangs touch her neck.

As her assailant drank, she and he became one for a moment; long enough that his cruel face nearly materialized in the mirror just before she died.

Whistling a discordant series of meaningless notes, DeWitt lit a candle, then looked around the great room to be sure he was alone. He still could barely believe his luck, and needed confirmation. Drawing the ring from his pocket, he admired it again in the candlelight. He quickly pocketed it as Zagarino appeared in the doorway with a short candle.

"Almost dark," Zagarino said evenly.

"...Yeah."

"Don't get them too close to the window," Zagarino warned, nodding at the candles.

"Right." DeWitt's nod was emphatic.

When Zagarino left, DeWitt once again brought out the ring. Sure he was alone for the nonce, he slipped it on, flexing his fingers, turning his hand in the candlelight. "Kiss my ring, you fool!" he commanded no one in a cartoon British accent, chuckling to himself with satisfaction. "Now, I...am The Master!"

The last sliver of the sun descended, leaving the room bathed in blood red darkness, a darkness so sudden and complete DeWitt spun toward the windows, envisioning some massive gargoyle-like creature spreading its wings across them.

He sighed, chuckling at himself. "Place must be gettin' to me..."

DeWitt tried to remove the ring - but could not. He tugged harder, harder still, till his middle knuckle cracked painfully, to no avail. "What the blue blazes?" He tugged fiercely at the ring, envisioning Bonner's rage, Zagarino's cold judgment. He panicked, looking around, sure that Zagarino would be there, watching him analytically-and offering no help.

"Damn!" he whispered, searching his dim surroundings for a solution"...Soap and water..." He hastily made for the kitchen, focused entirely on his plight-and saw Bonner coming down the dark stairway.

Bonner immediately detected DeWitt's shady demeanor, saw the wild distress in his eyes. "DeWitt? Where you going?" With a yelp, DeWitt quickly hid his hand behind his back, jabbering "Oh! Hey Boss! Finished already?"

"...What?" asked Bonner, "What the hell's that supposed to mean?"

Bonner came to the bottom and blocked DeWitt, giving him an intimidating stare.

"Oh...nothing. Just on my way to the can," DeWitt laughed nervously. "'Scuse me..."

"Just a minute." Bonner put a firm, halting hand on DeWitt's quivering chest. "What's with you, DeWitt?"

"What do ya mean? Nothing, Vic."

"You're acting...fucked up."

"Nahh... I just...gotta pee."

Zagarino came in from the kitchen doorway, leaning against the wall to watch. "You look...guilty, DeWitt."

Bonner took on a look of furious realization. "You took a wad of money to play with, didn't ya, Dimwit?"

"No, no...C'mon, Chief. It's DE-Witt..."

Bonner gruffly turned DeWitt around and jerked his hand out from behind his back. DeWitt's squeal of fright was comical-but no one laughed.

The huge ring reflected candlelight in Bonner's angry eyes. "Where'd you get this?"

"I just...found it," DeWitt stammered.

Bonner's patience, fleetingly restored by the sex, had grown thin again. "WHERE, BITCH!?" he bellowed.

"Downstairs," DeWitt relented, "In the basement."

"Aah. So...it was just lying around down there? All by itself?" Bonner's irony couldn't be mistaken for sincerity, not even by DeWitt.

"Y...Yeah."

Bonner twisted DeWitt's wrist back on itself, forcing the small man to shrink even smaller to alleviate the pain. "You're gonna show me where you got that fucking ring, aren't you Dimwit?"

"Y...yeah, Boss. I will. But it's gonna freak you out, man."

"Oh yeah? How's that?"

"There's a coupla stiffs down there. I pulled it offa one of them."

"...What?" Bonner bore down on DeWitt's wrist, until he heard a satisfyingly compliant whimper. When DeWitt didn't retract the wild story, Bonner finally released him.

"Just layin' there, all peaceful," DeWitt explained, rubbing his wrist. "But dead as a Mastodon."

The reference, completely foreign to Bonner, further raised his ire. "...What the hell is that!?"

DeWitt began making an elephantine shape with his arms, struggling to describe the creature. "It's a big..."

Bonner cupped his meaty hand behind DeWitt's neck and pulled him nearly nose to nose. "What are you tryin' to pull, boy?"

"They're extinct," interjected Zagarino.

Bonner looked at Zagarino threateningly, annoyed at having been educated.

"I'm not pullin' nothin'," DeWitt swore, "I'll show you!"

He turned sharply to DeWitt. "I'm gonna go get the bitch. Then we're all gonna get some shit straight about who's in charge, right?"

DeWitt nodded rapidly. Zagarino was still. "Don't move, Dimwit," Bonner ordered. As he stomped back up the stairs, Zagarino stared coldly at DeWitt.

Bonner found the door slightly ajar. With a healthy, long-nurtured sense of paranoia, he drew his .45 as he pushed it open just enough to step in sideways. "MaryAnn!" he called.

Looking around the candlelit room, he saw only the disheveled bed they had used. "Where the fuck..?" then, he spotted a blackish puddle on the rug in front of the dresser. "Damn. I musta really put it to..."

He trailed off, as his eyes fell to a finger poking out from under the bed. "What the hell are you doing?" Bonner growled, tucking his handgun into his waistband. "No games, babe. Get your ass out of there. You get to see the money now."

Receiving no response, Bonner lost his patience. "Dammit, you're all gonna learn to…" He reached under the bed and snatched her wrist. He dragged her halfway out - but something was wrong.

Her face was ash-grey, her eyes closed peacefully--but her mouth was open in what could looked like a frozen scream. "Maryann! What are you playing?" He smacked her on the cheek.

She lay pale and still.

"Shit!" Bonner gasped, pushing himself away from her. Then he noticed a pool of blood spreading under her back. Bonner roughly raised her corpse, looking around her. Her back was a crimson cavern, a red-edged void left by the brutal extraction of her heart.

Bonner scrambled up and dashed out.

Bonner came down stairs in a full-on sprint, alarming DeWitt and Zagarino. His gaze darted behind him up the stairs, then back at his partners. He had a look of wild fright they had never seen on him--and it was infectious.

"What's wrong boss?" DeWitt asked.

Bonner just stared at them, trying to focus past the mental image of his dead moll.

"Where's the girl?" Zagarino asked.

Bonner wiped his sweaty face with a trembling hand, then drew his handgun with a sudden jerky movement and jammed the muzzle upward against DeWitt's nose, making him look piggish. He took DeWitt's gun from his waistband and shoved it into his own, his eyes darting distrustfully between accomplices. DeWitt huffed a meek protest.

"Let's all just take a trip to the basement," he finally said. "You lead the way, Zagarino."

"What's the problem?" asked Zagarino.

"Shut up. And start walking."

Zagarino clicked on the flashlight--now flickering thanks to DeWitt's clumsiness, and went to the basement door. He opened it and descended first, followed by DeWitt, pushed along by Bonner. They all stopped to take in what meager detail they could in the dark stairwell, Zagarino shaking the flashlight frequently whenever the bulb dimmed.

"Shit...it sure got dark," DeWitt noted.

"Hurry up," grumbled Bonner, giving DeWitt another shove, almost making him stumble. They stopped again at the bottom of the stairs.

"Now, motherfucker," Bonner began, "Where the fuck are those bodies you were puking about?"

"...Over there, I think." DeWitt gestured. Zagarino shone the flashlight in that direction. The weak beam landed on the two boxes, casting odd shadows all around them.

"See!? There they are! Go ahead and look." DeWitt issued tiny nervous chuckles of relief and vindication. His relief died when Bonner cast upon him the hard look that was his default expression. "You go." Bonner shoved him. "Open 'em up."

DeWitt mustered courage, looking back to be sure his accomplices didn't bolt on him as he would have done, like thirteen-year-old boys playing a game of dare. He took two tentative steps toward the boxes, trying to keep his breathing steady, then closed his eyes and crossed the rest of the distance in two long, fleetingly brave strides. He stopped at the first one, gulped as he opened his eyes, and reached for it. As he gently opened it, Bonner moved backward just slightly, leaving Zagarino in front. DeWitt muscled the lid open—and gasped when he leaned down slightly to look. "What..?" He took out a zippo and sparked it, leaning in for a closer look. He dropped the lid with a startling bang, the hope of vindication far from his features. "Shit!"

DeWitt ran to the other box and quickly opened it. He needed only a split second- then dropped the lid and backed away. "Oh no. Oh shit fucking no. This is too freaky."

Bonner grabbed him by the collar and jabbed the .45 into his belly. "What the hell is this, douchebag?"

"Somebody moved 'em!! I swear they were there!

Zagarino shook the flashlight to give it more juice, then shone it directly into DeWitt's eyes. "All right. What'd they look like?"

"Like...movie stars or something. Nice clothes, jewelry." DeWitt held up his finger with the ring, as if this was proof. "The guy was blonde. The chick had long black hair, nice tits." DeWitt's brief leer was even more distasteful in the flashlight beam. "She was hot."

"How convenient." Zagarino swung the flashlight around to reveal the portrait—and the couple DeWitt had just described.

Bonner turned to DeWitt, furious. "That's it. You're gonna be the only corpse in that damn box, Dimwit." Bonner brought the gun to DeWitt's forehead. "Sweet dreams, sugar pie." DeWitt squeezed his eyes shut, gulping, sure he had reached the end of Bonner's fuse, and his own life.

"*Wait,*" whispered Zagarino, further raising Bonner's ire.

"...What!?" yelled the gang leader.

Zagarino didn't say anything for a long strange moment. "...Did you hear something?"

Bonner and DeWitt watched as Zagarino directed the light into the dusty darkness to their left, taking a tentative step.

In a micro-second, he disappeared into the blackness, like nothing more than a scrap of paper sucked into a vacuum.

The flashlight fell again, its lens and bulb shattering completely this time, as Zagarino screamed in terror for a split-second--then went dead silent. Whimpering, DeWitt grabbed and hugged Bonner tightly in the near-total silent darkness. For once, Bonner didn't protest.

"...Zag..?" Bonner called with a meek, shaking voice, "Zag!"

This quiet black moment was nearly enough to destroy Bonner's sanity. He suddenly shoved DeWitt away and let loose a roar of rage as he fired off two cacophonous rounds-- briefly illuminating two approaching figures with each muzzle flash.

DeWitt hid behind Bonner. "It's them!" he cried, "Oh God, they're-" Bonner spun and grabbed DeWitt, shoving him toward the figures. DeWitt screamed in terror, trying to stop his forward momentum. But long-taloned, clutching fingers caught him by the neck and moved him about with ease, leaving him disoriented.

Screaming, Bonner darted up the stairs and slammed the basement door.

A vague light grew in front of the terrified DeWitt's face, illuminating the source of the bear-trap grip on his throat. He beheld with utter paralyzed despair the glowing amber eyes of the towering male figure at the end of the steely arm, and the two gleaming-white spikes protruding from under his black grinning lips.

The Master's eyes became brighter. Looking into them, DeWitt saw the flames of hell.

"Mortals. Your short-sighted values confound me," noted the vampire with a voice that carried the weight of hundreds years of detached observation. The Master grasped DeWitt's ring finger, and savagely wrenched it off. DeWitt screamed and fought, essaying clumsy and ineffectual kicks at The Master.

He struggled to turn his head and neck out of The Master's crushing grip, but when he did, he saw the female vampire standing inches away, her blouse still undone. She watched his spouting finger hungrily, her almost feline features twisted into a smile of sadistic glee.

The male vampire released DeWitt, allowing him to fall to his knees, where he clutched his bleeding hand, beside himself with pain and shock. The blonde dead man slid his ring off the detached finger, licking blood from inside its rim before polishing it with a silk kerchief. He tossed the finger over his shoulder and turned to his expectant mate. "You may have him, my love."

She hissed, a primal and ferocious sound. DeWitt screamed again, one last time, as she lunged at him with fangs bared.

His eyes wide in the candlelight, Bonner watched the basement door as he reloaded the .45's magazine with shaking hands, dropping a couple of rounds when he heard DeWitt's death cry. For a fleeting moment, he had thought somewhere in the back of his mind that the guards would come along any second and break up this ruckus with their batons and hoses. Then he remembered he was far from the blessed safety of prison.

He managed to gather the shells in his trembling, sweaty paw and shoved the last of them into the clip just as the basement door slammed open.

He raised the gun toward the black rectangle of the doorway, waiting, holding his breath. But his assailants, he now understood, had all the time in the world.

It was DeWitt who emerged from the blackness, staring at him with a sick and frightened expression, bracing himself against the doorway. After a moment's rest, he took a step forward, the candlelight revealing a ghastly pallor in his face—and a gushing stump at his shoulder; his left arm had been torn away.

DeWitt stumbled toward his leader and friend, and collapsed at his feet.

"Son of a bitch!" cried Bonner.

He listened for footsteps on the stairs, but there was only heavy silence under the weak whimpering made by DeWitt. Staring over the top of the .45, Bonner saw the form of The Master take shape amid the shadows. Smiling, the dead man stepped aside to make way for his feral mate.

She parted her lips slowly to show off her gleaming fangs, and issued a menacing low purr, like a big cat, her slender right arm playfully held behind her back. In her left hand, she held the pearl necklace DeWitt had stolen. She handed it to her husband, as she raised what she was hiding—DeWitt's severed arm.

She arched her head back seductively to pour blood from the arm into her open mouth, allowing it to drip onto her tongue and down her neck and exposed breasts with an orgasmic rolling of her eyes.

Bonner had little faith in his gun left, but kept it trained on the vampires nonetheless. Old habits died hard for Bonner, just as he himself would. "You...sick motherfuckers!" he screamed, feeling for the only time some small empathy for the shivering dying DeWitt.

He opened fire--but his last hope dissipated like the paraffin vapors rising from the ancient candles. Even if his aim was good, the bullets had no effect. The duo of bloodsuckers simply stared at him, studying him, enjoying their game.

"You keep the hell away from me!" Bonner cried.

"On the contrary," the sinister blonde man said, "Hell is very close, my friend."

Bonner turned the empty gun over and swung it like a hammer, charging to strike The Master, again and again and again, without effect. The grinning vampire caught Bonner's wrist as he attempted a fourth blow, grasping him by the throat with his free hand and lifting him into the air. Bonner struggled, tearing at the tailored sleeve of his slayer's shirt.

The blonde man shifted his grip, snapping Bonner's neck in mid-air. Now paralyzed, the once-feared, dangerously violent criminal fell limp, save for his terrified rolling eyes.

"...Oh God..."

"We decided on Hell," corrected The Master. "Remember?"

The Master pulled Bonner close and widened his grin to sink his fangs into the exposed jugular. Bonner's lips quivered as he was emptied.

Zagarino emerged from the shadows, coldly watching his former partner's death throes; giving Bonner one last confirmation of his belief in a cold, cruel world. He calmly took a seat, lighting a cigar older than himself from a candle flame, as the raven-haired vampiress went to her husband's side, accepting a blood-filled kiss before gnawing into Bonner's wrist in feral manner.

Zagarino's cigar, a gift from The Master, was the best he had ever smoked. He sucked it as the vampires sucked the fading Bonner's blood.

He had a beautifully macabre, candlelit two minutes or so to bask in how he had beaten the system, before, the vampires finally turned from their bloodfeast in union to turn their eldritch amber stare to him.

The male flung Bonner's body to the side and daintily wiped the corners of his mouth, while the female by contrast, carelessly ignored the crimson mess that stained her face and breasts. Finally, she buttoned her blouse.

Zagarino found their pale, ancient beauty to be enchanting—but their gaze was unsettling. "A nice partnership, wouldn't you say? I supply the victims for you and make a few bucks for myself. I must say, it's been exciting." Zagarino rolled the cigar, letting the sweetish aroma waft about his nostrils. "Now, I'll just go and retrieve the money."

The two vampires shared a knowing look. The female turned to Zagarino, hunger dancing with candlelight in her sinister golden eyes.

"You won't need it." The Master intoned.

"...What?"

"You see, this arrangement has worked so well for us we've decided to extend it. Indefinitely." The candle behind him made a halo of his hair. But his eyes were like a tiger's.

Zagarino laughed uncomfortably. "What do you mean?"

The vampires didn't feel a need to elaborate.

"Come on, you've just had three...meals, hand-delivered to you," Zagarino stammered, "You didn't even have to leave your house. Surely, you'd agree that I...."

The Master interrupted with a baritone laugh, and a wink. "You've spoiled us, Mr. Zagarino. Thus, we plan to keep you around for a long time, to continue your good service..."

"I don't understand..." Zagarino said—though he did; beneath his fading state of denial.

"Half-dead, half-alive. How does that grab you?" The Master's fangs seemed to have grown longer since the brief conversation had begun. "Moving in places where we cannot. We like to call it a state of... apprenticeship."

Zagarino dropped the cigar to the floor, where its ember broke off and faded. "No, no, this wasn't the deal at all...No. You must honor our..."

But they had already begun taking steps toward him—or were they gliding? The candles seemed to be dimming.

"NOOOOOOO!" Zagarino screamed at the night, as the vampires came to loom over him.

In moments, the house stood quiet. Shadows moved gracefully within. Then the candles were snuffed.

***

Promises

Domyelle Rhyse

"He's dying." She watched surprise pool in Anthony's old, mud colored eyes.

"How do you know this?" Anger and suspicion, tangled with his possessive jealousy, chilled his voice, and Amelia resisted the desire to step back. She couldn't risk being locked away. Not now.

"You think I've learned nothing from you all these years?" She brushed her hair back over her shoulders, letting it fall into a stream of blue-black to her slim hips, with a hand too slender, too pale. "I want to go see him."

He glared. "You promised to remain with me, Amelia."

"And I have, and you spared his life. But now he's dying. I need to go to him." She softened her voice and knelt with her hands on his knees, pleading with the blue-gray eyes he claimed to love. "Anthony, please? I've stayed for so long, never seeing him, never going to him, not even asking about him, but always here with you, just like you wanted. Please let me go. Give us this one night."

He rose, his body lean and hard, and crossed to the window to peer out into the night. His porcelain skin paled in the moon's fullness, turning to unshadowed ice. "You wish to turn him."

"No!" She took a deep, ragged breath against the shock. After so many attempts to escape, to die, after forcing her to promise to stay with him by threatening Nathan, how could he believe she would want to bring the man she loved into this life? "No, I would never imprison Nathan this way."

Anthony turned and studied her, sucking her into the depths of his gaze. "You will return."

She heard the hint of desperation he tried to hide. Nodding, she kept her tone even, playing the game that had kept Nathan safe all these years. "I will return."

"Then go." A sly smile carved into his marble face. "Give him my regards."

She controlled her anger. Soon enough she would be free. But she couldn't leave him thinking he held the upper hand. "You may have stolen me from him, but he has always held my heart."

She left before he could respond, back stiff with her pride. There was only so much time before dawn, and she had to speak to Nathan before the sun rose. Taking nothing with her, not even a coat to ward off the new winter chill, she fled into the night, racing to the man she would have married if Anthony had not come into their lives.

Anthony. Pale skin, cinnamon hair, regal, flawless, amusing for the first few hours of their acquaintance with him. They had met the night Nathan proposed, on the patio of a tiny bistro. So many had come up to congratulate them, strangers who showered them with well wishes. Anthony waited until the crowd dissipated and ended up spending most of the evening with them. That was a part of his power. He became woven into the moment, subduing all objections without a single word.

He had taken her while they danced, one cool hand in hers, the other wrapped around her slender body, and promised to leave her fiancé alone only if she stayed with him. To keep Nathan safe, she had given her word.

But it was a hard promise to keep. Amelia was unsuited to the life Anthony had given her, the blood distasteful, and she missed Nathan more than the beating of her now still heart. She tried to starve herself, but he threatened her beloved, warned her that death would not save her lover. She had given in, hoping to keep herself pure from what she had become, always knowing that Nathan's natural death would release her.

The biting air scraped against her skin, but it was nothing against the desire, the need, to get to Nathan. She reached the rest home just shy of midnight. Age and despair touched the sick-laden air surrounding the low, red brick building, bringing a sour taste to her mouth. She stood in the shadows of an old oak, hesitant, uncertain. Nathan would be over 90 now. Did she want to see him elderly and weak, or did she want to remember him as the man she had said yes to on a cool, spring night? She wandered the yard, seeking his scent, stopping outside his window when she still didn't have an answer.

Her last memory of him was the night Anthony had found them. Handsome despite his too large ears--he kept them hidden under his thick, ash-blonde hair. His eyes, a hazel green, always hard to meet in their intensity, had been one of the first things to draw her to him. She could feel his calloused fingertips and smooth palms sliding over her skin, sending a shiver through her the like of which she hadn't felt in years.

It didn't matter if she saw him now. What could have been, should have been, would remain with her forever.

His window was open and easy to climb through. The room faced away from the east and lay in darkness, a tomb but for the breath of air the open window allowed. The breeze even washed away the medicinal scent, for which Amelia was grateful. Unpleasant when she was a human, the smell was vile to her more sensitive senses. She slipped quietly to his bedside and listened to his shallow breathing and the hiss of oxygen being pumped into him.

"Lia?" His voice wavered with age, but some of what he had been remained. The soothing deepness of it, like a rich, dark coffee, relaxing, comfortable.

She pulled up a chair and sank into it, amazed, fighting tears of joy. "How did you know?"

"You still smell of lilacs." He swallowed. "I'm dreaming."

"No, my love, I'm here." She took his hand and caressed her cheek with it. The soft crinkled flesh and thin bones felt nothing like the strong hands she remembered.

But, then, her own hands were as cold as the grave now.

"You're still alive?" He struggled to sit up but she placed a palm against his chest to restrain him.

"Yes." *If you can call this living.*

"Are you still...with him?"

The pain in his voice was a stake to her heart. "Only to protect you, my love."

"He threatened me?"

She nodded before remembering that he couldn't see in the shades of night like she could. "When he first turned me--"

"Turned?"

She hesitated before answering, slowly, carefully choosing every word. "Anthony is a vampire, Nathan, and has made me into one as well. I know they are things of legends, monsters in horror shows, but...they're real, and now I'm one of them."

"Oh, Lia."

The soft grief in the words echoed in her heart. She tried to continue, but the words tangled in her throat, and it took her several minutes to untangle them. "I tried to starve myself. I would have run into the sun, but he locked me away like some treasure only he should be allowed to see." She wrapped her cold, strong hands around his frail, warm one. "When he brought me the blood, I would wait for him to leave me then pour it out the barred window. He realized what I was doing, he warned me...."

A true death is leaving me more surely than fleeing from me. If you were to run, I would at least have the pleasure of hunting you down, trapping you, and choosing what to do with you. True death takes you beyond my reach, and places your Nathan in my hands. You made a promise, and only complete faithfulness to that promise will save him.

"You promised to stay with him?"

"For you, my love, so you would live." The tremor in her voice didn't--couldn't--scratch the surface of the agony of that decision.

"I wouldn't have asked for such a thing from you." He sounded querulous, angry. And old.

"No, and I would never have asked it from you." She brushed his cheek with her hand. "But that is love. It gives what must be given even if not asked for."

"And have you become the beast he made you to be?"

Amelia sighed. How to answer him? Had she killed? Yes, but not for many years now. She knew the signs of her hunger before they became her being. And she regretted every death; they pained her more than anything other than being parted from Nathan.

"I...I don't think so."

Silence ticked past them, each second another they could never regain.

"My love...I've tried--"

His voice turned gentle. "I know you would have, Lia. I grieve for who you were, who we could have been together. Every day without you was a day that was incomplete."

She smiled. "You always were charming."

"But it's the truth."

"You married, had children."

"I loved Marie, but she wasn't you. You're a part of me, always have been. I both hoped you lived and dreaded it...dreaded what he might have done to you." He disengaged his hands from hers and caressed her cheek. "What happens when I die?"

"I'll be free. My promise to stay with him was to protect you, if you're dead there's nothing left to protect."

"My children!" He gasped and the anxious fluttering of his heartbeat pressed against her ears.

"Have had children of their own, who have also had children. You are everywhere, my love. Your legacy is forever protected. Anthony has no interest in your scattered descendants, and he knows not one of them could hold me to him." She didn't add that Anthony believed Nathan's death made her his until he chose to release her.

Nathan stilled, his breathing so shallow she worried he had slipped away before all could be said.

His hand gently squeezed hers. "How did you know?"

"I've kept watch over you. Anthony allows his harem to have servants just in case we need protecting and he can't reach us. I knew when you married, was even given pictures." Embarrassment crept over her. "I cried. You were such a handsome groom." She hurried on before he could reply, not wanting to dwell on the loss. "I knew when each child was born. Elizabeth was beautiful, and I'm honored you named your youngest for me. Did Marie know?"

"I think she suspected, but know? I don't think so."

They let a comfortable silence pass between them and, for a short time, Amelia could almost imagine them together again. Young, ready to marry, more in love than anyone had a right to be. His aged voice shattered the illusion.

"Are you here to make me a vampire too?" Fear whispered through his words.

She dropped his hand as if burned. "No! Why would I turn you when I spent so long preventing such harm? "

His fingers sought hers, the tips rough with the memory of the calluses he'd once had. "To keep the promise we made before he came and destroyed our future, so we could be together forever."

The memory was one of her few joys, a treasure she had polished time and time again over the years. On a beach under a sky filled with the gems of the universe, they had promised to always be together. It was her last memory of him without Anthony. She lowered her head, resting it on his arm, grateful when his other hand caressed her hair.

"I can't do this to you, Nathan. I love you too much." And hate this life too much. Even your presence would not lessen the pain enough to make it bearable.

The relief in his voice echoed the sadness in hers. "I know." The pause sprawled across a lifetime. "What will you do when I'm gone?"

"I will join you. We'll be together once more. When the dawn comes, I won't hide. I'll let it lead my spirit to yours."

"And if he tries to prevent you?"

"He'll hold nothing over me ever again." She kissed his hand. "It's time for our vow to be fulfilled, and I swear it will be."

"I long for that time."

She held back her tears and whispered, "As do I."

The moonlight dripped over the windowsill, giving the room a faint light. He turned his face to see her and amazement passed over it.

"You haven't changed in seventy years!"

She smiled, comforted by the familiarity hidden in the folds of his own face. "Neither have you."

He laughed the laugh of a young man who had seen his beloved, and they talked of his life. Amelia enjoyed the little things she hadn't been told and shared what she knew of his descendants. The years melted away and they became young lovers once more, the lives they spoke of belonging to other people. Everything was said, everything shared. She lay her head on his shoulder, taking comfort in his arms for the last time.

Sometime before dawn, his breath left him, his heart stilled, but the joy of seeing her again remained on his face. She kissed his cooling lips and strayed out the window, waiting only to be sure that he would be cared for. She watched the nurses and doctors try to return him from death with no success, watched as they finally covered his face.

She didn't wait for the sun but found shelter and let her grief carry her into the daysleep. When she awoke, she fed, she wandered, she drifted in the sea of the night, searching for what she didn't know. Two nights later she found his grave. Her waiting was over.

Kneeling, she smelled the lilacs that lay like a blanket over the fresh earth, and caressed the simple headstone. "They've done well for you, my love."

And what will you do when I am gone?

"I'm coming to be with you. I promised."

"Can you keep your promises without another to force you?" asked a voice filled with the age of generations.

"Go away, Anthony, you're not welcome here." The dust of grief and anger turned her words hard and brittle.

"I hoped seeing him old and dying would show you the life I have given you, what I saved you from." His words grew slowly louder. No other sound accompanied his approach.

She rose and faced him. "I promised to remain with you so you would cause him no harm. Now he's beyond your reach and a promise forced isn't a promise at all."

He snarled, the smooth face turning feral when his fangs were revealed. "Such deception in you. You are mine and only I can free you."

"I am my own, regardless of what you made me. I will not stay with you again." She waved a hand. "Go back to your newest conquest. What was her name? Letisha? Your first African queen, you called her. You don't need me. Leave me alone."

"And what will you do without me?" His eyes narrowed.

"Fulfill a promise freely given long before you ruined our lives."

"You can keep no more promises to him. Return to me." He stretched out a narrow hand, pale in the glimmering moonlight. "I kept my word, now fulfill yours even if poorly given."

"No." A promise forced is no promise at all. You may have given yours by your own will; but mine wasn't.

"Amelia...."

"No!"

The burning hatred and anger in her voice made him step back. Stillness passed between them while he studied her. This time she avoided his eyes, knowing their danger and refusing to be mired in them ever again.

"Very well, Amelia, but I will give you nothing more, neither shelter when the sun rises nor food when your hunts fail. You are completely on your own."

He vanished, or so it appeared; he moved far too quickly for even her supernatural sight to follow. Such was the power of the ancient. For a moment, for less than a heartbeat, she felt abandoned.

No. This was her choice.

"I will need nothing from you," she whispered into the breeze, not knowing if he remained close enough to hear. "I have a promise to keep."

She knelt by Nathan's grave and waited for the sun to consume her. She ignored the hunger that pinched at her. She would not need food. The night passed slowly, and she let the few memories of their short time together help her pass the time as she waited. The day they met he'd come in for a tutoring session...ten minutes late. It didn't take her long to learn that late was the one constant of his life, and waiting had become hers.

Chuckling softly, she whispered, "And now you're the one who waits. Soon, my love, soon."

It began as a twitch in the middle of her back. Amelia straightened and rolled her shoulders, trying to relax and soothe away the persistent spasm. It only spread. Taking a deep breath, she forced herself to remain beside his grave.

"I will die next to you, no place else."

Tiny, insect claws crawled up her back, digging into her flesh. She shivered despite being far too hot, and wrapped her arms around Nathan's gravestone, using it as a shield against the quiet fear growing inside her. Her skin felt feverish, as if the rising sun was infecting her, making her ill. The sky lightened and the crawling became an itch that sank under her skin, making her insides shiver uncontrollably. She had to get up, had to move around, had to do something.

She stood and paced. Soon now there would be no escape. The sun would come and she would burn, her spirit rising with her ashes on the wind to join his. As long as she stayed here for a little longer. His grave was far from any haven, staying would leave her no options but to remain until it was over. The need to run quickened her feet, but she resisted the need, determined to stay near her beloved.

Amelia stopped. She stood in a clear well of grass, not a single headstone near her. How had she gotten so far from Nathan's grave? Panic set in. She needed to be near Nathan. Where was he?

She searched for his headstone in the growing heat, frantic, terrified she had lost him, but her eyesight blurred and reddened. There! She tried walking towards the block of gray marble. The heat resisted her, weakened her muscles, and still she clawed her way forward, desperate to reach him. She stumbled over something, and stared at the stone under her feet.

Nathan Edwardson.

She fell to her knees and clung to the headstone, soaking in the coolness of it. This, this was her freedom, her salvation. A fire started somewhere in her lower spine and flared, spreading over her back. The taste of ash filled her mouth, searing pain raced through her muscles.

Hang on. Just hang on.

What was she doing?

Keeping a promise!

Was she really? Would she really go to be with Nathan if she killed herself, or would she just be another lost soul, never reunited with Nathan?

Did she take the risk?

Molten pain flowed through her, overwhelming her other senses. She couldn't feel the breeze in the cool morning air, smell the flowers on Nathan's grave. The birds had fallen silent, leaving her deaf. Even the ashes no longer clogged her mouth. All there was, all she had, was the fire. The world burned around her, and she needed to escape.

You promised. Even if you're not with Nathan, you can at least be free of this monster you've become.

She was standing again, looking down at the red blur that was Nathan's grave. If she left now, she would have just enough time to escape the cresting sun.

But, Nathan. She had promised. And leaving would make Anthony better than her. He kept his promise.

The sky lightened. Time was running out.

Nathan.

The fire.

Pain raged around her, dripped from her fingers as she caressed her love's grave. She wanted, needed, to be with him again. Pain seared her heart, seared the edges of her will, burned away her promises.

"I love you!" she screamed. "I want to be with you forever!" She wiped blood and ashes from her eyes. "But I can't. I'm not strong enough. I'm not ready to die. Wait for me, my love. Wait for me with your Marie. I will come when I'm ready." Her voice dropped to a whisper. "I swear it on our love. We will be together again."

She brushed the grave with fingers of ash and flame and fled the coming daylight.

***

Ye Who Enter Here, Be Damned

Billie Sue Mosiman

As he opened his eyes the dark thickened, and grew as black as the bottom of a barrel. He lay in the depths of a grave. Swaddled in rotting clothing from a former century, his long nails clawed patiently at the shredded satin padding of the coffin. He had been at it even in his sleep-dream.

His heart beat slow as an African drum he'd heard once as a young man in Uganda. It came from a tribe he stalked, a group of primitives who wore carved sticks over their penises and sported black tattoos on their shoulders. He had drained dozens of them before he was done. The memory of blood made him lick his lips. His stomach was flat, his veins collapsed, but his brain festered with atoms sparking and igniting in the center of each brain cell.

Now he listened to his heartbeat, as he clawed away stinking satin and clots of cotton stuffing pressing down inches above his head. Only when he was free and fulfilled would his heart beat with new energy enough to carry him through into the future.

They had pushed the stake through his unholy heart, but as soon as they closed the coffin lid he'd withdrawn it. It had taken every ounce of his remaining strength. The pain, excruciating, left him faint and weak. But not dead. It had taken nearly a hundred years for the damage to correct itself, for it was his black heart that propelled him. With it punctured he had lain like the corpse they thought him for years, dreaming.

His nails reached the wood of the lid, having gotten through the batting. He methodically scratched at it, imagining it clarified butter, imagining it as cloud. The wood gave and rained down bits of damp splinters onto his chest. Finally earth filtered through the cracks. It smelled rank and full of worms, fertile as a river delta. He forced his right forefinger nail into the split wood and pushed it down and down, widening the gulf between him and the ground holding him hostage.

He came forth in darkness -a lucky matter for him. He hadn't seen the sun for a hundred years, even as a shadow cast on a wall. That great orb's beam would have rendered him blind for some time. It was not always true they could not take the sunlight. He was a creature living beyond all myths, even the deadly stake through his heart.

He sat beside his own grave, noting they had left a stone marker holding a warning: DO NOT ENTER HERE, FOR THERE BE DRAGONS.

He smiled. He was more powerful than any dragon and longer-lived, for the dragons had long gone from the earth even before mankind swam through the mud puddles as tadpoles.

He raised his head to see the moon and it was full. He arched his neck, letting the light bathe him in silver essence, renewing his soul. For he did indeed have a soul, though a black one. It responded to the celestial body circling the earth to bring reflected sun to those like him, who could not bear the brighter star for too long at a time.

He stood, shucking the tatters of his suit, leaving him a skeletal and naked man. He brought up his hands and ran his fingers through long raven hair, knocking loose dirt. He brushed his face down and clapped his hands to be rid of what earth still clung to him.

He put a hand over his heart, judged it strong enough to animate him for at least a while more, and set off into a lope out of the lost graveyard for the plantation house belonging to his murderer.

He -Charles Highgood -would not still be alive. No. It had been too many decades and taken him too long to release himself from the deep grave. But Highgood's descendants...they might still be in the big house, unaware he was coming.

For he was coming.

She was just a teen, not nearly yet grown. She lay beneath a sheet in the summer night, her window open to a breeze. He removed the screen and climbed inside the bedroom. He came to her bedside, staring down at the face flush with blood and life. He studied her trying to see some resemblance to Charles Highgood, the man burned into his memory. He couldn't make a judgment.

It didn't matter in the least, for this moment he needed her for sustenance whether she was a descendent or not.

He leaned over her and took her pale throat in his hands, his nails piercing two deep holes on the side of her neck nearest him. She woke, struggled, her eyes those of all men and women in the throes of drastic and violent sudden death. Not a sound escaped her throat. He put his thick lips over the piercings and began to take her down to the dregs of life.

Her legs beat at the mattress, the sounds bantam-like and of little moment. Finally even that effort at refusal ended. She lay in his hands with her head hanging back limply. He placed her against the pillow. Not a drop of her blood had spotted the bed, nor would it, for he possessed it all.

He felt the roar of her warm life renewing him in every cell, but most importantly he felt it plump his shriveled, repaired heart.

He tore the sheet from her dead body and wrapped it around his nakedness. It would serve until he found something to wear. He cared little about his nakedness, but didn't want to be caught out that way, making him more vulnerable to excuse for his existence.

The next night, after a day hiding in the deep woods near the family graveyard, he came again. He had seen the distraught family on the grounds of the plantation. They met two police cruisers, and escorted officers into their fine old home.

A funeral ambulance came and took away the girl. It was long and black and spoke of calm reverence for the dead.

It would come again and again, if he had his way. And he would.

The second foray into the plantation house found him in an empty bedroom going through a closet. He found suits, shirts, shoes, and belts. He selected a black suit as shiny as shark skin, a long-sleeved shirt white as early dawn. He dressed quickly, relishing the feel of silky material against his cold flesh. He had washed himself in a stream so that now his long clean hair fell in wavelets to his shoulders. He was rather vain and knew it, but it was said he had been an extremely handsome man in his day. His nose was aristocratic, the planes of his cheeks high, his lips full and sardonic. He could mesmerize humans before he was even close enough to put them into trance with his deep-set dark eyes. They saw him coming and fell in love with his presence. He had missed that adulation so much! Men were such pitiful beings living superficial and luckless lives. He gave them, at least for a short while, a feeling of worship for that which is greater than they could possibly ever become. He was mankind's god. They were all his children.

He turned in the floor-length mirror and looked at himself in the shadowy room. He looked like a groom on his wedding day. His hair shined, his eyes were deep pools of wisdom and knowledge, his lithe frame was straight and strong. He was more beautiful than an angel of death might ever hope to be.

That night he slipped in each bedroom and sipped from every member of the household. There were six of them in the house, all connected by blood. He could taste it. One of them tasted better than the others and he wondered at that. He looked down at the sleeping man and adored him. It took nothing for him to control his hunger, and a good thing or he would have taken this flavorful meal fully. He didn't yet want to dispatch more victims until he had discovered the true facts of their heritage.

On the third night he knocked at the door. A young man opened it and his eyes widened perceptibly at the dark stranger standing on the threshold. "Sir?"

"I would like to see the master of the house. My name is Fitzgerald Comis." It was old language, he saw that the minute he said the words, but the boy was well-mannered in the Southern tradition and asked him inside to wait a moment.

A middle-aged, pot-bellied man wearing dark slacks and a blue shirt came to the door. "How do you do?" He extended a manicured hand. "I'm Benjamin Highgood, how may I help you?" This was the tasty parcel he'd sampled the night before. Saliva rushed into his mouth and he had to swallow noisily.

The name - Highgood - exploded like a wild stallion in the old vampire's brain. They had kept the ancient place in the family just as he'd hoped. That's really all he needed to know, but he smiled congenially and said, "I'm doing some research in the parish for my book on old families from the Civil War and wondered if you'd have a few minutes to indulge me."

It was hardly past dark and it appeared Benjamin Highgood was a loquacious man who had never met a stranger. He escorted Fitzgerald to a parlor where they sat on opposite horsehair Victorian sofas to speak softly about the past. Unlike his ancestor, Charles, there didn't seem to be a suspicious bone in the man's body. He spoke of the killing fields and the buried Confederates. He mentioned the little graveyard they'd begun on the property where they'd buried strangers and family alike.

The vampire guest pretended to take notes on a small pad he'd taken from a desk in the house the night before. He finally slid the pad into an inner jacket pocket and stood to leave. "I want to thank you for your time, Mr. Highgood. It's been generous of you."

Once outside, he turned and looked up at the three-story edifice, his sense of smell telling him where all the Highgoods were located and in what rooms. He'd wait until after midnight and then he'd make short work of them.

All of them.

He went from room to room, a wraith of darkness sucking life from woman, man, and child alike. He was unmerciful, full of blood and black rage, each life entering him a reminder of the years spent locked in the grave, waiting for a time of renewal. Did the Highgoods think they could make an end of him? Did they think they were rid of the demon who had walked these Louisiana woods and lands for hundreds of years?

He saved Benjamin for last, as the man had been the one earlier in the night who had hosted him and given him the reasons for the massacre. He was also the one whose blood was the sweetest. He wanted him to know the others were gone - all because of him and his trusting nature.

He slid into the bedroom where the man slept alone. He was unmarried, brother to Kane Highgood, the married older brother who actually owned the plantation house. The one lying dead and sprawled on the floor next to his wife in an upper bedroom.

Fitzgerald saw a pillar of dark on the bed and it sat upright. He paused, holding perfectly still.

"You won't have me," Benjamin said. He threw back the covers and stood from the bed. He seemed taller, wider.

"So you know what I am."

"Not only that, but I know *who* you are. My great grandfather put you into the ground where you were supposed to stay all eternity. We have a daguerreotype of you I've studied for years to memorize the look of you. I knew you the second I saw you at my door tonight. I know you've tasted me as you did all the others. But you won't take all of me."

Benjamin flicked on the bedside lamp and Fitzgerald flinched.

"I've taken the others," Fitzgerald said. His mouth was blood-stained and his long fangs lay over his bottom lip. He hissed and balled his fists.

"You've done me a favor. I would have done it myself, as they were useless to me, but suspicion would have fallen on my shoulders. Now I have a murderer to parade before the authorities."

"You can't chain me or hold me."

"We held you before - in the grave - and I am my great grandfather's son."

With that Benjamin Highgood flew through the air, moving as a blur, and landed on top of the old vampire, driving him to the floor. He was at his neck, clamping his long fangs into the carotid artery. Fitzgerald fought mightily. The two of them, locked in battle, were flung from floor to ceiling to wall. Lamps tumbled, chests fell over, windows burst outward.

It took a great deal of time and effort. Benjamin was not as old a creature as was his nemesis, but his strength was legendary among the new vampires in the parish. He had never lost a fight and he didn't lose this one.

He now lay atop the vampire dressed in his father's clothes. The monster was not dead, but he was too weak to move a muscle. Only his eyes moved in their sockets, his rage a whirlwind spinning crazily as he looked to the left, the right, and up at his captor.

Benjamin rose and went to his bed. He reached beneath it to the floor and brought out a sharp wooden stake and a sledge hammer. He kneeled and pounded the point into the old heart. Blood spewed, covering Benjamin, the floor, and the near wall. The old vampire lay still, staring. Then Benjamin took the monster's right hand, pounding it free from the body with the hammer until the bones liquefied and the muscles were strings. He tore it free from the forearm.

The dying vampire thought...he thought...*I will pull out the stake again. I will regrow my hand. I will return one day. Doesn't he know that?*

Benjamin carried the corpse down the stairs and out the front door onto the verandah. He paused, staring up at the moon and stars. Soon it would be morning.

He lay the body on the ground and stooped to light several pieces of his clothes on fire. The flames danced lightly as if licking the body, until they merged and were a conflagration. The body lay motionless, but the mind in the body screamed in horror, screamed in howling pain and rising fear.

Morning brought the sun and as Benjamin sat on the porch steps in the shade watching the pile of ashes, he saw the first rays strike it and send it spinning into the wind, disintegrating the last of the vampire forever.

Inside he called the police to report the deaths of his entire family. He had attacked the killer, he said, and beat off one of his hands.

When they arrived and saw the dead bodies and the strange, long-nailed hand lying in a puddle of blood on Benjamin's bedroom floor, they were shocked and revolted. The sheriff said, "God, Mr. Highgood, I've never seen anything like this. Where do you think the intruder went? Surely he would have bled to death losing his hand this way."

"He ran from the house and disappeared in the woods. Maybe someone will find him some day lying in the swamps."

The funeral home sent five cars to carry away the dead. The murders were a source of talk for months between the locals in the parish. Some of them took the word of the last surviving Highgood about what happened. Others whispered of graves left yawning and the walking dead.

The plantation prospered over the next hundred years despite the fact Benjamin Highgood never married, and one day when he might have been in his eighties, Benjamin simply disappeared never to be seen again. A new family bought the plantation and refurbished the old home, spiffing it up with paint and a new roof. One day they employed an old middle-aged man with a pot-belly and thinning hair who called himself Benji. He was to keep the grounds mowed and the gardens groomed.

"Love this place," Benji said to the new owner one day as he raked autumn leaves into a pile. "It's as if I've always been here."

"Yes, it is nice, isn't it? You know about the carnage done here years ago, the family found dead in their beds?"

"I might have heard the rumor."

"They say they were drained of blood and there was a clawed hand of the killer left behind on the floor of the master bedroom."

"Oh, I wouldn't count on old tales being absolutely truthful," Benji said, his eyes twinkling. "It's just stories."

The man nodded thoughtfully as he walked away to leave his groundskeeper to his business.

Far off from the house in the old family graveyard five bodies stirred in their caskets in the earth. Each had a stake through the heart and each had withdrawn them with great effort and immense determination.

The Highgoods all began to scratch against the casket lids with long, clawed hands...

***

The Blood Runs Strong

Chantal Noordeloos

"It is all about blood," the Master preached to his followers, who kneeled around a stone casket, dressed in grey hooded robes. Their heads bowed in reverence.

"The blood gives us strength, it gives us power. The blood runs strong."

"The blood runs strong." The followers hummed in agreement, their voices echoed slightly through the damp cold tomb.

One of the robed figures moved towards him and kneeled, head still bowed. Delicate white hands presented the Master an ornate silver ceremonial knife. He took the slender blade from her hand, and touched it to his lips, the cold silver a stark contrast with the warmth of his skin; then he returned the knife to her hands.

"Master. My blood is your blood," a husky female voice said. One dainty hand took the knife and cut into the soft white flesh of the opposite palm. Her blood welled up from the cut, gathering in a dark pool in the center of the palm. Several drops escaped, trailed down the pale arm and disappeared in the wide sleeve of the robe. She offered him the blood covered hand, and with a cruel smile he bit into her flesh, sinking his sharp teeth further into the skin. He could hear a slight hiss as she inhaled from the pain, but she was brave and loyal. When he was done, he licked the blood off with his rough tongue. He released her hand, the blood still specked on his lips, and she recoiled slightly. The Master licked his lips, and the hooded girl handed the knife to another of the followers. The ritual repeated itself. Each time a new subject would offer a bleeding hand.

He spoke to them, his words filled with fire, his message was about blood and death. As he spoke he directed his face towards the light of the many candles, so that the sharp canines in his mouth glistened. He was aware of his body, and every move he made, every word he said, was deliberate. The followers chanted the words of the ritual in his name, chanted praise for the blood, and - he imagined - dreamt of immortality.

The ritual ended in darkness, the many candles that illuminated the tomb were extinguished, casting the interior of the stone building in pitch black. Only the musty smell of ancient stone and death remained, and a vague odor of the extinguished candles.

The Master made his exit from the tomb with two females, one clung to each of his arms. The air outside was fresh and cold. A million bright stars greeted them from a velvet sky.

"Draco," said one of the girls. "Will you take us home with you tonight?"

He looked down on her. His eyes glanced over the vivid red hair with dark roots showing underneath. She was a short girl with small breasts; her body was lithe and thin, resembling that of a young boy.

"I will take you home with me." He spoke with an accent, which he hoped was Transylvanian.

It wasn't the accent Draco was born with. Then again, Draco wasn't his real name either. His real name was Ewan Holister, and he was born in some little redneck town to the south. Back in that town he had a bad reputation; he was a weird little boy who liked to torture animals. Bigger children bullied him for being a 'freak', and they liked to beat him until his pale skin was covered in bruises.

Now things were different. Here, in the city, he was Draco, a tall and handsome man whom people called Master. During his early twenties, when his awkward body matured, Ewan realized he wasn't the same creepy child; that in fact he was quite handsome.

When his grandmother died – the old woman left him a considerable sum of money. He moved away from the bland little town when he was twenty one, determined to create a new life for himself. His good looks opened new doors for him. He trained his body at the gym, and his mind at the library, because with strength came power. The tormented little boy who grew up miles to the south, died then, and Ewan –who was now Draco- vowed that he would never be weak again. He would give the word 'freak' a new meaning.

He dyed his long brown hair black, and was meticulous about keeping his roots in check. He changed his wardrobe from jeans and t-shirts to black leather trousers and black pirate shirts. He invested his grandmother's money and lived in a cheap apartment on the outskirts of the city. He would spend his time frequenting gothic clubs, and managed to build an air of mystery about him. Draco would stay in the darkest corners where he simply observed the people around him. He perused books and articles about the personality archetypes, and found he was a master at studying the human character.

People were drawn to his mystery and Draco was inspired by their desire for him.

Then the rumors began.

He heard whispers that some thought he was a vampire. The thought turned him on and so he indulged himself in the fantasy of being a real life vampire.

When one of his investments paid off nicely, Draco bought himself a pair of dental implants. Two canines, a little longer and sharper than human teeth, and his transformation was complete. As a vampire he drew even more followers, all eager to be near such an elusive creature.

His followers were loyal; they would all offer their blood, and probably their life for him. They called him Master and played his game. He held weekly rituals and demanded sacrifices of his followers. They would shower him with money and gifts. Draco wanted for nothing, and yet... as the years grew on the sacrifice of his followers wasn't enough to satisfy him anymore; he grew hungry for something darker.

Somewhere inside him, that little boy Ewan wasn't as dead as he thought him to be. That little boy longed for the pain he caused the animals that he tormented; he demanded more than tribute blood. Draco's heart housed a monstrous anger towards the human race, and the thought of suffering pleased him.

Draco was building an army of followers, and he was preparing them for something far more than silly little rituals —those were only to get them used to the blood- he had a grander scheme in mind. He was preparing his flock for greatness. After all, being a vampire was all about the blood.

The girls giggled and rubbed themselves up against him as he led them to his most recent abode. They were eager. A little too eager. Draco fantasized about dragging them into his house, kicking and screaming.

The thought of their resistance aroused him more than the sight of the two women undressing in his velvet black and red bedroom. They put on quite a show for him. One of the girls - who gave herself a silly name like Letitia - used a razor to make small cuts on the other girl's stark naked body. She in turn screamed with pleasure and pain. The lily white skin was decorated with long streams of blood, and Draco felt himself grow hard at the sight of the blood and the pain. She offered her soft curved flesh for him to lick clean with his tongue. He obliged with a reserved eagerness, keeping his cool as he let his taste buds savor the metallic taste. The tip of his tongue followed the blood down, and he ran his moist hot mouth over her thigh. With sharp teeth he bit her flesh, right next to a wound he had made a few days earlier. The girl screamed, but there was no fear in her voice, only delight. He bit and licked and the girl moaned. *Soon I will find a real victim. One that will fear for her life, and I will ravish her and take her life's blood.* His time was coming, the time to make the transition to a real hunter. Some of his followers were ready. If this was a success, he would find himself a fresh victim every week, and feast on the blood.

The more he drank, the more he was convinced the blood made him stronger. Though he was born human, he was truly a creature of the night, and the blood would help him in his final transformation to immortality. Perhaps if he took a life, he would transcend to a new physical being.

Murder kills the human soul. He read that somewhere, and he liked it. *I have no need for a human soul, nor for humanity. I am a new creature. I am vampire. My blood runs strong.*

The girl wiggled under his mouth and tongue and for a moment he thought about puncturing her femoral artery and letting her life juice gush over his face and chin. He pictured taking her through the blood and watching the life seep slowly from her eyes.

Not this girl, not one of my own flock. I will find another.

Draco slid inside the willing young woman and thought about who he would bring along on his hunt. Who would get the privilege of sharing his first kill?

The night was nearing its end, and the club was starting to empty. The smell of sweat and stale beer seemed more prominent now that the masses weren't there to drown it out with perfume and other scents. Draco sat in his usual spot, surrounded by two of his followers. Jake - who was now Edmund - and Isaac, who did not feel the need to change his name. They were loyal, but that is not why Draco picked them to join him on this hunt. He picked them because they were cruel.

Edmund was a mountain of a man, his formidable muscles stretched his shirt. It was rare for a Goth to be so well built, but Draco suspected that Edmund was too much of a coward to be around men of equal strength. There was something strangely feminine about Edmund, and the way he treated women. Draco believed he had been damaged by a female at a very young age. It was something they never spoke about, but Draco liked using his follower's weaknesses against them. Whatever happened to Edmund in his childhood, it primed him to be cruel and strong, just like Draco was. But still obedient, and afraid to be out in the world on his own.

Isaac was different. He was small and aggressive in a way only a short man could be. Isaac compensated for his insecurities about his stature with a big mouth and a rotten attitude. It made him hot headed and dangerous, and that was just what Draco liked about him.

It had been a slow night - too many girls travelled in large groups, or were with boyfriends - but as the night progressed and the patrons moved on to another club or went home, Draco spotted the perfect victims.

Two girls sat at one of the booths, and were drinking in silence. The men who approached them were turned away with a word or a glance. They were both very beautiful in their own way. One had dark, long, straight hair and skin the color of light caramel. No makeup tainted her face - she was the only one in this place that appeared au naturale. Her face at least - Draco could not see what she was hiding under her jeans or the plain red t-shirt she wore. The girl next to her was a different matter. She was a Goth from the tips of her black and purple dreadlocks to the soles of her knee-high laced-up boots. Her face was accentuated with dark makeup, which made her look almost feline, and several silver piercings protruded from her skin.

"I have found our victims," Draco said. It was the first thing he had said all night. He liked being mysterious, and mysterious men weren't chatty. With an easy grace and confidence he walked towards the women, his two followers in tow. *I will charm these two bitches to death.*

"Good evening ladies." Draco leaned forward and made a small, almost imperceptible, bow. To his amazement he saw the girl with the long brown hair roll her eyes at him. In the dim light he could see they were an unnatural shade of green. *Contact lenses, so she isn't that pure after all.* "I am called Draco, and these are my companions Edmund and Isaac. May I inquire your names?"

It was the Goth girl who spoke, the other one just stared at him in solemn silence.

"My name is Ophelia, and my friend's name is Thalia." Draco looked at the girl with the dark makeup and realized she too was wearing contacts. Purple.

"What beautiful names." Draco tried to lift the hand of Thalia. *This one I need to convince. The other is already mine.* He felt the soft skin of the small slender hand, and noticed how warm she felt. The clubs were always stifling, and most people were bothered by the heat. Draco was good with heat; where he was born and raised, the summers got hot.

"Listen," Thalia said with a bored expression on her pretty face, "can we just skip this little song and dance? We'll go straight for the part where my friend and I tell you that we aren't interested." Her fingers played with the rim of her drink, and she looked Draco straight in the eye.

Draco felt his blood turn to ice, and he struggled to wipe the incredulous look off his face. *Who does this bitch think she is?* "Ladies," he said, smiling. "I did not mean to offend..."

"You didn't. We are simply not interested. Have a lovely evening." She didn't even look at him this time, she looked straight ahead and sipped her drink. "Go away, please."

Arrogant cunt. Now the blood boiled inside him, and he knew he was going to enjoy ripping this bitch apart. Isaac moved a little forward and he hung over the table of the booth.

"What's the matter, bitch? You think you are too good for us?"

"I do, but that is neither here nor there," the woman answered. Her friend laughed softly. "I just want to be left alone and I am fed up with men like you hitting on us." She turned to Ophelia. "Unless you are interested?"

The other girl shook her head. Thalia looked back at Isaac and shrugged. "See? We both just simply aren't interested."

"Are you a lesbian?" He leaned over towards her, fists knuckle down on the table, his face filled with rage.

"Would that make you go away?" Thalia asked with an infuriating calm. "Because, then, I would *gladly* be a lesbian".

Draco watched Isaac and Thalia converse in silence. He would not interfere, this woman was unafraid and neither his charm nor his intimidation skills would work on her; he would look a fool. Isaac's eyes widened a little. Then he leaned in, squinted and curled his top lip in a sneer.

"You know what I think?" The vein on Isaac's forehead throbbed visibly.

"Enlighten me." The woman's voice a bored monotone.

"I *think,* you're a little whore, who is playing hard to get," he hissed between his teeth as he leaned over the table towards Thalia.

A lesser woman would have shied away, but this bitch just sat and continued her eye contact with a bemused look. *That is the most fearless woman I have ever met,* Draco thought with more contempt than admiration.

"I think the whole point of being a 'little whore' is not to play hard to get," she said, one eyebrow raised. "Playing hard to get wouldn't exactly make me a lot of money, would it? And seeing as I haven't solicited you for any money, we can assume it is my night off from 'whoring'." She paused briefly and shot Isaac a look worthy of a schoolteacher, showing an insolent pupil the error of his ways.

Then she raised the glass to her lips again, and speaking over the rim, she said: "So I kindly ask you, and your friends, to get on your way, and leave us alone. We are not interested in your company." Thalia took a small sip from her drink, and gave him a warm, almost convincing, smile.

"Fuck you, you uppity bitch," Isaac hissed. His flat hand hit the table with a loud meaty smack. "I'll be seeing you and your little Goth friend later." He lifted his hand from the table and pointed two fingers first to his own eyes and then to Thalia.

She held his eye; her smile never wavered.

Draco shot the women another look; he smiled exposing his teeth. There was something in her face that pleased him. It was shock, and probably fear. He turned his gaze away from her and passed the table as if he never stopped in the first place. *We will see you later indeed.* He felt annoyed that Isaac gave this woman so much power, by acting the fool. But his fuelled anger would come in handy later, and Draco was curious to see what an infuriated Isaac would do to this woman. *I can taste your blood already, ladies.*

"What is it about you that pisses people off so much?" He heard the Goth girl ask her friend as he walked passed.

"Confidence," Thalia responded.

"He's going to try and hurt you, you know?"

"I know."

They waited for the girls in the alley near the bar. Draco hid in the shadows, dark and deadly. His heart pounded with a loud rhythm, but he kept his face still, devoid of any emotion. Isaac was different, he was riled up. He was pacing and muttering softly to himself. Edmund looked a little pale around the nose, and Draco wondered if he had underestimated the big man. *Will he prove to be unworthy?* He never had the chance to finish the thought, because Isaac spotted the two women. Before Draco could hold back his minion, Isaac shot out of the alley.

"Oh look, it's the lesbian whore and her little Goth friend," Isaac said in a sharp voice. Draco saw the Goth girl look at the other, but her friend's face betrayed nothing.

Draco motioned for Edmund to flank the girls and he walked out of the alley to stand in front of them.

"Our situation hasn't changed," Thalia said. She didn't turn around to face Isaac as she spoke. "We are still not interested".

"See, you want to know what I think?" Isaac said as he shot back a nasty grin.

"I have some suspicions of what goes on in a mind such as yours." Thalia retorted.

The short man ignored her. "I think that you need to be taken by a real man."

"Oh, do I now?" Thalia laughed. "Well I guess I will have to go and find a real man. Good night to you, Gentlemen."

Draco and Edmund cut off their path. Ophelia closed her eyes and sighed. She looked miserable, and Draco liked that.

"I'm afraid we shan't let you leave, ladies. We have unfinished business." Draco leaned against the brick wall of a building with lazy confidence.

"I think the five of us are going to have a real good time together," Isaac said.

Draco shot him a warning look. It was time for Isaac to go back in his pen, and let the master take over.

"You do a lot of thinking for such an ignorant little man" Thalia said sharply to Isaac, and the short man looked as if he wanted to attack, but he looked at Draco and backed off.

"It's not nice to insult my minions," Draco said, and he flashed her a smile that revealed the sharp teeth.

The girl looked at him with a faint hint of surprise.

Now I have your attention, don't I, Girly? He felt a mad rush of power.

"We are going to have a little fun together, the three of us and the two of you. I'm afraid you won't be going home, tonight. Or ever again. I am too *hungry* to let you go home." He looked at his fingernails and then glanced over his hand at her. "When I am done having my wicked way with you, I will let my friends have a turn, and then I will eat you all up. You see, the five of us are going to have some fun." He snapped his teeth at her to emphasize his words. He wanted to taste the fear in her blood.

Thalia turned to him and folded her arms. She leaned a little on her right leg, which made her left hip stand out, there was something in her face that Draco did not like. The Goth girl just looked like a frightened mouse.

"Sir, I do believe you have challenged me," Thalia said. Something in her eyes shone, and she took off the leather jacket that she wore.

"Thalia, don't," the Goth girl pleaded. "You'll get in trouble again."

"I think I have a good excuse," Thalia explained with a chilly calm. "The man threatened to rape and eat me. That would make what I am about to do, self-defense." Draco felt his confidence wane. *Who does this bitch think she is?*

"Thalia, please," Ophelia begged. It was obviously pointless, the other woman gave Draco a long hard stare.

Before Draco could react, the woman moved with a speed that his human eyes could not keep up with. She actually blurred from his vision. The blur moved first past Edmund, who fell to the ground with a heavy thud, and it stopped near Isaac. The little man's eyes went wide and he doubled over. What seemed to be a shadow moved around him, hitting him, and Isaac moved with every blow. Draco was reminded of the invisible man stories he watched on television as a young boy, as Isaac received punches from an invisible foe. Then he fell to his knees, and his body toppled over forward, his cheek making audible contact with the cobblestone street. Draco looked at his fallen comrades, fear crawling in his belly like a tarantula in a nest. Both his followers were alive, but their injuries prevented them from getting to their feet. Soft groans echoed through the silence in the alley.

Thalia stood in the middle of the alley, amidst his fallen minions. Her attention was now turned to him. There was a change in dynamics. Draco pressed his back against the cold brick wall, his eyes searching around for escape. *Who the fuck is this bitch? What is she?*

The woman walked towards him with slow deliberate steps. Draco thought she looked bigger now, as if she grew somehow. Now she was the hunter, and he was her prey.

He took a step sideways, the roughness of the bricks scraping against his shirt. *What the fuck is happening?*

Suddenly Thalia was upon him. Her arm shot out with uncanny speed. A steel grip wrapped itself around his neck and Draco felt himself being lifted off the ground. He struggled to catch his breath, his hands clutched at her arm to keep the weight off his throat. Tears welled up in his eyes and he gargled.

"I agree, this *is* fun," Thalia said quietly, but with enough menace, that Draco felt the hot urine spread down his leg inside of his leather trousers. The smell of ammonia tickled his senses. "Want to show me your pointy teeth again?" He wanted to shake his head, but couldn't. Without warning the woman flung him across alley, where his back collided with a sickly crunch against the brick wall. The air was knocked from his lungs, he slid down the wall and fell to the ground like a sorry sack of potatoes, and landed on his hands and knees. The skin on his palms and his knees tore, and thick blood welled to the surface. Draco could barely comprehend what was happening to him. The woman –Thalia- was hovering over him. *How can she be so fast?*

"You said something about having your wicked way with me?"

"Please," he begged. "I didn't mean it." Tears streamed from his eyes, and they mingled with snot and saliva that poured from his nose and mouth. Draco pushed himself up a little from the ground, he turned his head to his attacker and showed her his fear and desperation.

"You wanted to *eat* me now, didn't you?" She squatted down in front of him, her eyes glowed an eerie green in the light of the street lantern. Draco shook his head, he wanted to deny it. His ribs hurt and he had trouble breathing. The woman punched him; she caught him on the nose and the upper lip. He could feel the bones splinter and his skin burst. Two of his teeth dislodged. A flame of red light overtook his vision and he fell hard to the ground. He coughed blood and broken teeth; one of them a dislodged fang. The impact was like being hit with a brick. He had never felt anything so painful. Through swelling eyes he saw her pull her arm back, ready for another blow. He sobbed.

"Are you planning to kill him?" It was the Ophelia who spoke.

Thalia froze.

Then Draco saw her muscles relax.

"He's an asshole, but that doesn't warrant a death penalty," Ophelia said. Her voice was soft and low, her eyes were still focused on Draco.

Thalia took a few deep breaths and then she shook her shoulders, as if shrugging off an unwanted garment. The smile on her face returned. "Just making sure none of these gentlemen will ever try to rape a woman again." Her eyes were hard as she spoke, she was almost gloating... almost.

"It's not really fair you know," he heard the Goth girl scoff. She nodded towards Draco and his fallen companions. "What? Where is the fun in that?" Thalia asked, her eyes round with childish innocence. She bent towards Draco.

"What do you think, Toothy?" she whispered. There was a cruelty in her green eyes. "Do you think I should have told you I was a vampire? Given you a fair chance to run?"

Draco shook his head. Not to answer her question, but to deny the situation all together.

"You look like you are going to eat him." The Goth girl sounded as if she were about to lose her patience. He couldn't quite see her through his swollen eyes, and Draco was afraid to look up.

"What? Gross. I don't eat humans. That's sick. They look like us." Thalia grimaced at Ophelia. "Next you will be accusing me of sucking on road kill. Don't *you* judge me for being a vampire."

She reached for something near Draco's face; he flinched at the hand that came so near.

"I think he filed his teeth or something. He had fangs."

"Fangs?" Ophelia's voice was high with surprise.

"Yes. Humans think vampires have fangs."

"He probably thought he looked like a vampire." The women laughed loud and harsh.

"Bless him." He could feel Thalia's hand tousle his hair and he curled up in a little ball. She got to her feet and took a step back from Draco's broken body.

"He looks pretty wounded." He heard the Goth girl come closer and he saw a shadow cast over him.

"We'll call an ambulance to pick them up. Let's just go before the police come."

Draco prayed for them to go. To leave him in the blood that was pouring from the various cuts on his body, nose and mouth.

"Take care now, *Fang boy*." Thalia's voice sounded harsh and mocking. "I hope I appeased your hunger."

"You really have a talent for attracting these weirdos." The girls' laughter slowly faded from the alley.

Draco ran his tongue across the bloody gaps in his gums. The taste of blood was conflicting. It reminded him of power, but now also of his own weakness. He thought about vampires and how stupid he had been to think he could ever be one.

There on the cold stones of the alley, Draco bled to death.

It was Ewan the paramedics put in the back of the ambulance. It was Ewan whose hunger had been stilled.

The blood runs strong. But not for me.

***

Blood Ties

Sarah I. Sellers

"Death has found me…" Toby whispered as shivers racked his small, malnourished form. The rain came down in sheets, wind blowing furiously, showing no mercy. The boy was obviously ill, with abnormally pale skin, his cheeks were gaunt, and his eyes almost life-less. He cowered in an alley, trying to escape the relentless storm. He was small for his nine years, and maybe forty pounds soaking wet.

"It is only me, young one," A man's voice, like gravel, rough and uninviting, startled Toby. A cold hand grabbed the boy's shoulder. A dark robe cloaked the man's body, and shaded his face. Rain seemed to avoid him, as if each drop feared the hooded monster.

"All things considered, you may wish for death to come next." He paused with a grin. "To hell with you!" He boomed with cruel laughter, tightening his grip on the boys shoulder. Toby cringed. Tears joined the rain cascading down his sunken cheeks. He coughed. His throat was dry, and his heart was beating rapidly.

"Why are you so cruel? Who are you" The boy's voice shook as he spoke, and he was trying not to look at the man who had tormented him relentlessly. He whispered horrid things about hell into Toby's ear and stabbed at him with bony fingers. Only when Toby slept did the jeering cease. Exhaustion had gotten him now, and he was slumped against the alley wall.

"That is of little consequence;" He sighed, "but you can call me Legna." He took a step away from Toby. "I knew there was something wrong with you. I never wanted-" he paused. "I saw that vile creature and I want no part of it."

Legna held up his cane and whispered into the air, "You're a monster, not a protector. And you cannot protect this one. He's not yours to protect." He spat the words. "Parasite."

As the cane struck his legs, Toby thought he felt a soft hand on his shoulder and was grateful he'd seen his friend this morning.

Everything went black and the pain was insufferable. This couldn't be death, Toby thought, for death would have been a gift. He felt as if his lungs were being torn from his chest while hands clutched at his throat. Toby was falling endlessly through the darkness. When he hit the solid ground, the impact didn't hurt as bad as it should have. His back only ached dully. He actually felt stronger; more alert. He felt... alive. Wherever he was, it was dark. Only the light of twin moons illuminated the gravel road.

He didn't know where he was or why, but he felt unusually calm, considering the circumstances. This was a strange place, somewhere other worldly. Toby felt Legna's presence before he heard his cane tapping the ground. His sense of calm vanished.

"Welcome to your new home," Legna cackled. His words sent shivers down Toby's spine. "You will soon meet your master." He tapped his cane menacingly on the ground, "Until then, stay put. Beasts dwell in this area. Beasts that will not hesitate to rip your head off." Then he vanished, not allowing the frightened boy to comment.

Under any other circumstance Toby would have fled, but here, in this unfamiliar place, he had no advantage. No familiar street corners or secret hiding places. He sat at the edge of the dirty road and cried. As a small consolation, Toby realized that he wasn't as skinny as he had been. He was still small, of course, but his skin didn't hang on his bones like it once had. His face and clothes were covered in grime from the city streets, but despite his exhaustion and some soreness, he felt better physically. He wasn't starving. The joy of this discovery didn't last long though. He still had no idea where he was or why. He cried himself to sleep in the dark of night, on the side of the road, in an alien world.

A tall figure approached Toby in the early dawn, as a purple glow came across the horizon. The world was just beginning to stir. The stranger, looming over the frail child, took a deep sigh and his broad shoulders fell. The tall man bent down and took the boy into his arms. Underworld dwellers watched as he carried the boy across town. It wasn't every day that their king, Lucifer, ran his own errands.

When Toby awoke he was pleased to feel a soft, silky fabric below him, but he was utterly confused. Why wasn't he outside? In his alley? Then he felt it; the unmistakable burning of eyes watching him from the darkness. He pulled the blanket closer and glanced around, his eyes straining to catch a glimpse of the watcher.

"Relax child." Unlike Legna's voice, this voice was smooth and deep, almost alluring. Toby's eyes widened. In the darkness surrounding him he could see nothing but a thin strip of light from under the door.

"You are right to fear me, as many do." The voice came again in a reassuring tone, but this time it was closer. Toby turned his head quickly to his left, to where he had guessed the man was, but only saw black. Then Toby was momentarily blinded when light flooded the room.

"Here, Toby." The man was right next to him now. Toby scrambled out of bed in the opposite direction and, then looked back. Dark red eyes, like soul-less voids of unforgiving sin, greeted Toby. The man smiled at the child on the floor, revealing pointed teeth. "You may call me Master. Nothing else." His red eyes trained on Toby's shocked form. "If you have nothing important to say, do not address me." He hesitated, then walked across the room and bent down to help the child up. Toby whimpered and flinched away.

"I wanna go home…" Toby cried, tears streaming down his face.

Lucifer hissed; he reached one finger over and wiped a tear away from the boy's face. He held it to his nose and sniffed cautiously. He placed his finger to his tongue and tasted the salty drop.

"It's a tear…" Toby whispered.

Lucifer growled. "I know what it is!"

Toby gasped and continued wiping away the tears. Lucifer softened and placed his hand on the boy's shoulder ever so briefly, and then was gone.

The following day Lucifer escorted Toby around the mansion. Toby could hear the servants whispering. Apparently this was not a task the King would normally take upon himself, but Lucifer was especially interested in this child.

After visiting the dungeons, a horrible place under the mansion filled with demons and half-dead men screaming in agony, they wandered back to the main floor. The rooms they passed were occupied by members of the Underworld committee or Lucifer's guard. Servants watched from the shadows as they toured the halls, until the odd couple reached Lucifer's quarters.

"No other servants are allowed in these rooms. This is my room. You only enter if I tell you that you may do so. You will clean this room only. You will also assist me with anything else that I might need." He stared at Toby.

"Why me?"

Lucifer glared now, his lip curled into a snarl like an angry animal. Toby stepped back.

"I could have sent my hounds to get you; you could be in the dungeon right now! Do not belittle my invitation! I brought you from the streets and into my home, you incredulous little bastard." Lucifer's eyes darkened to black, and his hands formed fists.

Toby glared. In a moment of courage, he stood all four-foot tall and stared Lucifer in his soulless eyes.

"I don't want to be here! I'd rather be in the dungeon!" The words left his mouth before he could comprehend what he was saying.

"Then I will banish you." Lucifer hissed in anger.

Toby vanished in a cloud of black smoke. Lucifer sat at the edge of his bed and sighed.

Toby couldn't see anything. He could feel chains at his wrists and ankles, and he was facing a wall. The pain came without warning. A whip came down with unrelenting force. Once, twice… it left a searing pain each time the leather struck. Toby cried out in agony, his screams echoing in the dark room and harmonizing with the screams of others. Tears streamed down his stained face. Preparing for another strike, he closed his eyes tightly.

"Enough, Marter."

Toby continued sobbing as the chains released him and he fell into Lucifer's arms.

Salma, the only healer in the Kingdom, stood as soon as the door opened and Lucifer entered, carrying the child. She rushed forward, ushering him to set the boy face-down on the hospital bed.

"Now get out." She glared at the surprised King. There was an unspoken battle in their eyes and then Lucifer turned and left.

Salma examined the young boy. His back was a mass of blood and torn flesh. She treated the wounds and then lifted the boy's shaggy black hair to look at his neck. There she found a deep burn; a symbol resembling the letter D.

Salma entered Lucifer's room without knocking. He was standing shirtless in front of the window, watching the two moons. He too had scars on his body, from a millennium of battles with the angels. She had never noticed how bad they were. He also had tattoos, one on his left bicep and one across his back. Both written in a language she did not recognize.

"Lucifer -" she hesitated. "The child has been marked."

After checking on the child, and seeing the mark for himself, Lucifer sat with Salma. "The war between angels and demons started at the beginning of time, Salma. I don't agree with God's criteria for Hell worthy sins. My demons survive on sin. More humans and their sinful souls go to Heaven for cleansing than they do to Hell for torture. And so, many demons have nothing to live on and eventually die off. I can't allow that." He shook his head. "God must lower the sin scale, to send me *all* the murderers, robbers, cheats, black magicians….I want them."

"So why can't you have them?"

"God thinks they can all be saved. We demons know that's not true. But we need something more. We've been fighting a losing battle for centuries."

"And we still don't know…" Salma pondered. "Why is Toby here?"

"I don't know. I found him on the road. I was intrigued. Children don't come to hell."

Frustrated, the King of the Underworld consulted one of his most ancient texts. The writing had become faded and worn, written well over two-thousand years ago. He found the symbol from the boy's neck and began to read aloud:

"While many believe these marks are given by the demons of the underworld, they are the actually the mark of a heavenly angel. The Angel Dayan marks the hybrid-human children of her angel sisters and brothers with this symbol, ensuring their protection. These children always have a guardian even if something happens to their human parent and their angel parent. They are to be protected at any cost by the angel kingdom.

"So why aren't they protecting Toby? Why did they leave him here? Knowing he'd likely be killed?"

Lucifer continued reading:

This symbol is also thought to tell the coming of the half-angel, half-demon child of Satan. The Vampire King.

He looked up into Salma's shocked face, "Because he's mine."

When Toby woke up the next morning, his back was sore and his stomach was growling.

"Morning, Toby," Salma's chipper tone broke the silence. "Are you ready for breakfast?"

He nodded politely and started to get up.

"No silly, you get it in bed!" She laughed, pushing him back down gently. Then Lucifer walked in with a tray in his hands. He awkwardly placed it on Toby's lap. Salma nodded with an encouraging smile and Lucifer cleared his throat.

"I hope you like it, Toby." Lucifer smiled lightly.

"Thanks, um, Master?" Toby hesitated, wiping the tears of gratitude that had fallen.

Lucifer looked at the crying boy, confusion and frustration beginning to cloud his face again.

"So, do you want to visit the town, Toby?" Salma nudged Lucifer's arm. Lucifer gave Salma a glare.

"Yes, Toby, would you like to visit town?" Lucifer mimicked, avoiding the child's bright blue eyes when he looked up.

"Um…" Toby let out a nervous cough and hesitated.

Lucifer sighed impatiently, tapping his foot, and scratching the back of his neck.

"Fine, we won't go." Lucifer hissed, turning around and exiting the room in a huff.

Salma sighed. "That man is spoiled. No patience and no regard for human life."

She smiled at Toby and patted his leg.

"I know what must be done." Lucifer sat in the corner of his chamber when Salma arrived.

"And what is that?"

"His angel side…the source of those tears – must go."

Salma looked concerned and then hopeful. "But we can keep him?"

Lucifer gave her a crooked smile.

"Toby!" Lucifer's voice echoed through the mansion, Toby jumped to attention, stumbling to the door. Lucifer was standing across the hall from Toby's room.

"We'll have a feast here tonight, and I expect you to be dressed and ready in twenty minutes. I do not want you to speak unless spoken to. We will entertain some of the highest members of the Underworld - besides myself of course." Toby nodded quietly, and did not move until Lucifer left the room. When he did turn around, a suit was laid out on his bed.

He was heading toward the suit when his friend, the one Legna had called "Parasite," manifested next to the bed, his body hunched over and his face contorted in pain, blood dripping out of his mouth and chest. He looked at Toby with glossy, bright orange eyes and snarled, showing elongated fangs. Toby withdrew and stifled a cry.

"Don't go to the dinner. It's a trap. The angels are-" And he vanished. Toby stood frozen, petrified. The door burst open and Lucifer scanned the room, his eyes landing on Toby's shivering form.

"Who was in here?" He asked. His nostrils flared. Toby didn't speak. Lucifer snapped twice and Toby was suddenly dressed in the fine suit. This broke Toby out of the shock. He began dry sobbing. Lucifer shook his head and led the boy out of the room and towards the dining room.

Despite their size and obvious power, the room full of demons still flinched when Lucifer and Toby entered.

"Hold your back straight and do not shrink from eye contact. These demons are important to what we must accomplish. You must learn to command authority."

As they sat, no voices filled the room; just forks and knives against plates and bowls. Eventually small talk began and there were murmurs all around the table. Once the food was served, the real conversation began. Lucifer was entertaining the group with the newest ways to torture a soul when the demon on his right took hold of his forearm.

"Did you think you could keep him from us, Lucifer?" Samuel asked, his head still down, looking at his plate.

Lucifer stopped and set his fork down.

"We need to destroy the beast." Samuel continued. "He will be the end of us. Including you."

Lucifer looked up from his plate slowly, confusion in his face, "I will decide-"

There was a loud boom and Toby was gone.

"Where is my son!" Lucifer roared, slamming his hands down on the table. "What is this treachery?"

"He is being taken to your dungeon where he will be decapitated and staked." Samuel smirked as he shed his disguise, exposing his angel form.

Lucifer let out a growl and lunged across the table. The other angels acted quickly, shedding their disguises and pulling Lucifer off of their leader.

Whispers and then screaming erupted from an empty place behind them. Then a blast of light and a loud crack.

Toby stood where the light had been. His eyes a deep maroon, fangs extended, blood dripping down his face, and the angel Legna's head in his hand.

"I want to stay here now," He hissed, "with my father."

Lucifer began laughing. The angels began to panic, then disappeared one by one. When only Samuel remained, Lucifer smirked and pulled Toby close to him.

"He is ours now. He has accepted his demon side. Go tell your God to prepare himself."

***

Born of the Earth

Justine Dimabayao

The pebbled balustrade is cool against my hands, which look ghostly against the moonlight. The moon at the zenith is waxing--due to reach fullness by tomorrow. Like myself, my family's vineyard--at least, what is left of it--is practically a ghost of its former self. The leaves have fallen, and the branches have shriveled up.

I close my eyes and inhale the nocturnal air. I could almost smell those fresh grapes as my family's employees picked them bunch by bunch. Then I imagine daylight glowing through my eyelids as I oversee this vineyard myself.

Mama would have been proud. Or perhaps not--she was conventional, to say the least.

My family ran a vineyard in Cotnari, Bukovina, and we were considerably wealthy. Being the only daughter among seven children, I had little idea of what was to become of me. My mother was contented with having a man to support her and sons to follow their father's footsteps. Unfortunately, I shared my brothers' adventurous spirit.

Time and again, I would listen in the shadows of our mansion as my oldest brothers bragged about how many women they had taken and the youngest ones dreamed about going across the Carpathian Mountains to see the rest of Romania and if they could, cross the Black Sea and explore Constantinople before sailing into the Aegean.

Every other time, my mother would find me in the hallway leading to the bar and reprimand me, claiming that what I heard from my brothers was not meant for a lady's ears. Often, she would pull me out of the dark and put me back in my bright bedroom. She would put me in front of the mirror and brush my luxuriant golden locks. In order to take my brothers' ambitions off my head, she would praise my beauty and call it my greatest asset.

"You are lucky, Aranka," she would tell me. "Most girls are happy to have one man running after them. But you will have many. You will be free to choose which one would make the best husband. He will provide for you, as your father has done for me. You will never have to work or worry. ...."

My mother's words were prophetic: as soon as I turned fifteen, boys of varying degrees of boldness offered me almost everything from love notes to jewelry in exchange for my attention and companionship. Having many suitors made me rather pleased with myself. For the first time, I truly acknowledged how beautiful I was. For once, my parents and the household servants weren't the only ones telling me so. No matter how much I dreaded seeing myself as a wife doing nothing but admire her husband's marvelous work, I liked being pampered. I delighted in being showered with gifts and compliments--by rich and handsome young men, no less.

In return, I did my best to be a respectable young lady. My mother taught me everything I needed to know about etiquette. Learning punctilious manners was exceedingly boring, but I practiced them all in my eagerness for favor. My father, on the other hand, valued intelligence as much as manners; he would instruct me to read one or two books every week. He would make me read everything from the Bible to Romantic novels. I found this activity surprisingly enjoyable. I liked reading anthologies of Slavic myths the most. Once or twice, when I would join my three youngest brothers in exploring the forest, I would imagine Rusalka[1] waiting for us in muddy ponds, or the hauntingly beautiful Iele[2] dancing among the trees. We were also careful not to stay out past sunset. Vampires were not easy to hide from; they were also talented shape-shifters; they could appear harmless or enticing if they pleased. They could appear as the mist settled on the forest floor, the shadows between the trees, or the bats hovering over our heads.

My brothers and I kept these outings a secret from our parents. I was not allowed on these little adventures. But my brothers let me accompany them because they were glad to have among them a woman who was not fussy and squeamish. Sometimes, they would even dress me as a man, so they would appear to have one of our servant boys with them while they would later lie that I was in the company of one of my suitors. While they hunted birds and beasts, I collected insects, lizards and beautiful stones. When my mother would find a small tank of plants and insects in my room, I would lie that a suitor had shared with me his passion for exotic creatures. She would always believe me; she probably thought: *She would never go into the woods, my young Aranka. It's not ladylike.*

I continued this routine until one day, it seemed I was paying for the lies I had told, and the secrets I kept. I was deathly ill of a strange affliction and none of the physicians my family hired could determine what was wrong with me. All they observed were two tiny puncture wounds on my

---

[1] Water demons; ghosts of maidens and/or children who died from drowning

[2] A trio of forest nymphs; they attack people who see them dancing.

throat and I couldn't explain where they came from. All I could tell my family was that I was fit as a fiddle one night and I was dreadfully weak the following morning.

Even my brothers felt guilty. Dénes, my youngest brother and best friend, gravely apologized for encouraging me to join them in the woods. The others agreed, believing that a forest being had laid a malevolent hand on me hoping to make me its slave when I die.

"That's ridiculous!" I shouted, frustrated that I couldn't leave the house. "The rest of you should be sick, too, if that is the case!"

No matter what had made me ill, there was no curing me. The wounds on my throat wouldn't heal. They appeared infected; the flesh around them turned white while the wounds themselves shrank, as if swollen from the inside. I turned hideously pale. I couldn't look in the mirror without crying. Dark circles appeared under my eyes. I looked like a living corpse with ugly marks on my neck.

After a few days, I could no longer get out of bed. I couldn't eat. I was very hungry, but nothing could satisfy me. What made it worse was that my stomach rejected everything I consumed. I would vomit even the freshest milk. This made me awfully irritable. In one fit of rage, I upset a tray of food before strangling young Kalyna, the maidservant. She could have died if Elek, my third oldest brother, hadn't rescued her. But when she reported that my face contorted beyond recognition and that I drooled while my teeth grew sharp, she was fired at once.

Nobody could explain the shift from extreme weakness to inhuman strength. Even I was becoming scared. I enjoyed flirting, but I had never entertained sexual fantasies. Now however, I dreamed of a faceless man soothing my wounded neck with his tongue. I could hear myself moaning softly, purring like a cat. I could feel my hands pressing against his bare back, my fingernails digging into his smooth, firm skin. When I awakened, I would find my hands tearing at my nightdress. I never told this to my family. But the secret only increased my bursts of rage.

By weeks end, I was sure I was going to die. My family knew it, too. They gathered around my bed, and one by one, my brothers kissed me goodbye. When it was Dénes' turn, I was suddenly overwhelmed. "I love you," I told him.

"I love you, too, my sister," he said, innocently.

When he leaned over to kiss my brow, I caught his intoxicating scent. He smelled like a brandy--only more powerful. Then, a beast was instantly roused in me. All reason and will was forgotten as I seized his head and locked my lips on his, pushing my tongue into his mouth. I wrapped my legs around his waist to keep him from breaking away. I needed to taste him. Nothing satisfied me the way his sweet, soft mouth did. Even his panic fueled me. I could feel his heart pounding against my breasts. I could hear his harsh breathing.

 The rest of my family was so alarmed they were frozen for a few long moments before pulling Dénes away from me. By the time he was rescued, I was so immensely satisfied that I laughed softly, gently gnawing my own knuckles, gratified by the shock on Dénes's face.

"What? Did you want more?" I teased.

Dénes never came near me again. The rest of my family guessed that what had happened was a momentary delirium that commonly occurs shortly before death. They loved me so much they were willing to lie to themselves.. I was disgusted, but I didn't have the heart to apologize to Dénes. What I felt was real. No good words or gestures could sugarcoat what I had done.

The day after, my family gathered in my room again. Dénes remained at the window, all the way across the room from me. To my horror, they brought Rosaries and crucifixes.

"Put those away!" I shrieked. "Get them away from me!"

Mother embraced me and told me to close my eyes. "We know you would be leaving us soon. We are praying for your soul, my darling," she told me. I held on to her, trying to ignore the holy words they were uttering. But by the middle of the Lord's Prayer, I was screaming of sheer terror. I felt like they were already killing me. Not knowing what was wrong, they recited the Prayer for the Dying.

"Stop it! Please, that's enough!" I begged, sobbing.

Disturbed by my behavior, they continued praying outside. My mother stayed with me to encourage me to eat. Again, I refused, knowing I would vomit whatever I tried to eat, even if it were water. So I slept, trying to endure the hunger. I closed my eyes, waiting to die.

When I awoke, I thought I had gone blind. Not even the vague moonlight graced my eyes. I tried to sit up, but my head bumped against solid wood. I reached out, touching only thick planks. Panic seized me, and I screamed and kicked, trying to destroy the coffin I had been caged in. *I'm not dead! I'm here, I'm still alive!*

It must have taken several minutes before I finally broke the planks. But that made earth cave in on me. I wasn't going to give up. I had to get out. Struggling to keep my eyes and mouth closed, I clawed through soil. The broken pieces of wood tore my clothes as I made my way upward. The will to live was the only thing keeping me from stopping. I tried to ignore the taste of dirt whenever I tried to breathe. After what felt like hours, I made it to the surface.

I shot one hand out, then the other. I pulled myself up. Spitting and coughing out earth, I racked my brains. What had happened to me? I looked around. The quarter moon shone brighter than usual upon the graveyard. The smell of soil and rot mingled strongly. My ears picked up the faintest human voices, which had to be at least a hundred feet away. Frogs and crickets called out so loudly it was as if they were all right next to me.

Then, I heard the most distinctive sound of all: the beating of a heart. I looked around, until I found a tall figure coming toward me, accompanied by a gentle sphere of light. Then, the scent of brandy drifted in the air. The memories that returned to me reminded me that I was still Aranka Ungur, daughter of Costin the winemaker.

"Are you alright, Miss?" the young man asked.

His scent wrapped around me, obscuring everything else. The only other thing I felt was my insides burning, begging for nourishment. My jaws ached dully, making my mouth water.

"Dénes," I uttered.

In my hunger, my voice sounded distant. But the sound of his name kept me conscious. I lifted my face. Indeed, it was him, my gentle younger brother, holding a lantern. As he had done that day, he looked upon me with stark alarm, his mouth open. I approached him, heedless of my filthy appearance and shredded white dress.

"I'm glad you're here," I whispered in his ear.

Dénes' eyes went wide with shock and I hooked my arms around his neck. It was when I opened my slobbering jaws that I felt his hands push forcibly against my chest. Weak in the knees with starvation, I was easily shoved away. I hit the ground and snarled at him. Then he raised the lantern high in the air.

I dodged the lantern as it crashed on the exact spot I had been and set it aflame. Screaming, I hid my face from the fire.

"Go away!" barked Dénes.

I glanced at him. To my horror, he was holding out a crucifix. I recognized it at once; our grandfather had given it to Dénes before he died. What strange power such an object had over me: like on that day when my family prayed for me, I felt like I was dying.

I roared at Dénes, but there was nothing else I could do. It was as if, aside from the fire, there was an invisible barrier around him that I couldn't penetrate.

"Go away!" repeated Dénes, stepping as close to me as he could, holding the image of Christ Crucified in front of me. That was when I couldn't stand it anymore. With a final growl at my brother, I fled as fast as I could from the flames and from the Cross.

I ran, aimlessly, through the graveyard, until I found myself under street lights. That was when I fell on all fours, unable to hold my own weight any longer. I listened to my own ragged breathing for a few minutes before my ears caught the sound of beating hearts again.

I turned to my right, where, from a short distance, a man and a woman holding hands were walking on unsteady feet. They were laughing and speaking in hushed tones. They abruptly stopped moving and talking when they spotted me, looking rather helpless on the pavement.

"Do I know you, darling?" asked the woman, who bent down and touched my bare shoulder. I caught the smell of liquor in her breath. At the same time, she shuddered and jerked her hand back. I didn't miss the unmistakable terror in her eyes when they took a closer look at my face.

"Whoever left you here must be a scoundrel ..." the man told me, gently but firmly holding me above the elbow.

With a deep breath, I gathered just enough energy to lift myself up and grasp his head. He had barely reacted when I sank my teeth through his throat, where the pulse was strongest.

The woman screamed. I couldn't let her call for help. Without letting go of the man's neck, I reached for her hair and tugged it down. I heard a faint crack before she fell on the pavement, motionless but conscious.

Thick, warm blood filled my mouth and soothed my throat. Finally, satisfaction--as the man's blood entered my system, his very vitality transferred to me. I grew stronger while he went limp. All that I had suffered was over. I owed this life to this peasant. What a shame he couldn't retrieve what he had shared.

I didn't stop feeding until the man's heart ceased beating. When he was dead, I carelessly dropped him, before descending on the woman, who was trapped in her paralysis.

With cold fascination, I listened to her asphyxiation while I sucked her sweet blood.

When I'd had my fill, I became drowsy. My vision swirled. However, the dizziness wasn't such a discomfort. Giggling, I stood and walked around the street, looking for a place to rest. I slowly made my way through the winding streets toward my family's vineyard. The grapes smelled wonderful, although not as appetizing to me as usual. I was well inside the garden when a cold hand gently touched my shoulder.

Behind me there stood a venerable older man and two enchantingly beautiful dark-haired women. They were all much taller than I was. The man was not remarkably handsome, but he looked dashing in his black cape and carried an air of reverence. His neatly combed mustache added a sophisticated touch to his look. His cold *red* eyes should have been frightening, to say the least, but I felt no fear.

He smiled widely at me, revealing nearly his entire set of teeth, all white and gleaming, complete with a pair of prominent canines.

"Come, my dear," he told me in a clear, deep voice. "Daylight is coming in a few hours. ... Wandering around is not safe."

"I'm not wandering," I argued, confused. "I'm going home. My family lives here."

When I turned my back on them, one of the women took my hand.

"No, darling," she said. "You can no longer go back. We are your family now."

I bit my lip, unwilling or unable, to protest. Moonlight shone on my hands, spotted with dust and blood.

I was not the same girl I had been before.

I remembered clawing my way out of the grave. I remembered how my beloved brother had turned me away.

As I looked at the expectant faces of these strangers, I realized I didn't belong to my old family, or their customs, anymore. I bowed my head in acceptance and embraced my freedom; hand-in-hand we walked away from the vineyard.

***

Shattering Glass

Brian D. Mazur

It was the second time that Harry Kirkland's life had changed; it was also the last. It began with a knock at the door as he sat watching the news, a human-interest story. The knock was light, but authoritative. It was a small hand he decided, shuffling to the door.

Rap music boomed from somewhere in the condominium complex, greeting Harry and ushering in a pair of women standing on his front stoop. The older of the two was an attractive woman, about thirty-five or so, he guessed. Her brown hair, short, swept across her forehead, trimmed neatly framed around ears that displayed silver earrings in the shape of feathers that sparkled in the setting sun. She wore a dress brushed with the colors of the rainbow. Her eyes were emerald green and she greeted Harry through a Mary Tyler Moore smile with big gleaming teeth.

Next to her stood a young woman, about the older woman's height, but not so effervescent in her appearance. She was thin, hollow cheeked, rather morose as she stared at

Harry with dull, lifeless eyes. Her hair was straight, dull brown, well past her shoulders, lying lightly on a dress that was too big and seemed as if it should have the same design as her companion's, but like her, lacked color, life. She hung on almost desperately to the older woman, her right arm intertwined with the woman's left, hand clutched tightly into her companions until her knuckles were white, her left hand grasping the woman's upper arm.

Harry thought that he'd seen them before.

"Hello," the older woman said, brightly, her free arm extended in greeting. "My name is Jennifer Warston. This is my daughter Melissa. We moved into the complex a short time ago. We've been so busy that we haven't had time to introduce ourselves."

Harry realized that he was still staring at the young woman. He found that looking into Melissa's eyes a little longer that, yes, he *had* seen them before. They'd moved in about three months back. It was as if they were just suddenly here. There had been no moving van of any kind. None of the activity normally associated with moving. They had just been . . . here.

"I'm sorry. Harry Kirkland." He shook her hand. "Welcome to the neighborhood. Actually, I think that introductions should have been my responsibility. I *have* seen you and your daughter around but neglected to introduce myself."

She didn't respond, only smiling a very pretty smile.

"Won't you come in for a moment?" he stepped back and swung the door open wider. "If you don't mind the bachelor's ambiance that . . ."

Jennifer shook her head vigorously, her earrings dancing with slivers of sunlight off its metal.

"No, no, no, thank you anyway. Melissa and I have to get to the grocery store. We just came by to introduce ourselves and to invite you to dinner tomorrow night at our place. Number twenty-four." She turned and pointed back across the court.

Harry glanced quickly to Melissa, who was staring blindly, still clutching at her mother as if she were about to be taken away forever. He looked back to Jennifer who was still smiling.

"Can you make it, Harry?"

Harry considered the invitation for a moment and the twinge of guilt that rode with his thoughts. He hadn't realized his devotion to Lois was still so strong, but there it was.

It came at first, the changing of his life, in total silence. It greeted him, as he stood in the entranceway of the old Victorian, unmoving; the house vibrating with what was *not* in the air. When he came home, he would always hear Lois singing in the kitchen as she cooked. That night being their fortieth anniversary, he had expected her to be singing loud and clear with that alto warbling voice of hers.

"Lois?" he called out.

He placed his lunch bag on the little table between the umbrella stand and a fifty-year-old cherry wood coat tree. His gaze skidded along the immaculately polished wood floor of the short hallway ahead, to the kitchen door at the end. A yellowish white glow around the doorjamb reflected white pools on the floor and on the thirty years of memories that covered the walls on either side.

He stepped forward with some hesitation. Something wasn't right. It was too quiet.

"Lois?" he whispered.

He placed a hand on the door and stopped. He was afraid of what might be on the other side. He felt the grooves of the wood grain under his fingertips. He had no reason for this panic, it just emanated deep within him, causing a great stillness in his heart.

When he entered the kitchen, the first things he saw were red grapes, some cut in half, some not, spilled from a bowl across the white veneer of the kitchen table. One of the chairs lay on its side, Lois next to it on the clay-colored tile, with a smattering of the grapes around her. The knife she'd been using, its black handle slick with sticky grape juice was just out of the reach of her stained fingertips.

He knew that she was dead.

There would be no warmth in the soft hands that he so often held in his calloused ones. Her eyes, those sparkling blues that he never, ever grew tired of looking into, would be staring blankly to the ceiling fan above the table. He knew all this even before he knelt down to her.

His stomach tightened, his throat constricted. He felt outside of himself. This was somebody else here, somebody else at his feet. Lois would come dancing through the door behind him singing, "Helloooooo, Harryyyyyyyyyy!" followed by the usual hug.

Kneeling next to her, he very gently gripped her by the shoulders. He ran a hand gently through her salt and pepper hair. So soft, clean, but messed up from the fall, not as perfect as it usually was. He did the best he could to place the hairs back to where they should be.

He pulled himself together enough to dial 911. He did not pay heed to the police and paramedics when they arrived, or when someone placed a blanket around his shoulders; nor did he pay attention when they offered words of comfort before pulling him away from Lois, as strangers surrounded her.

Two days later the doctor said something about a weak spot in Lois' brain. On the day of her funeral he said his last goodbye after everyone else had departed. He talked to her about selling the house and moving to Florida, just as they had always discussed. He explained that he simply could not live in that house without her.

The house sold easily enough. A young couple, much like Harry and Lois thirty years earlier, looking to start their lives together. It was the perfect place, Harry told them.

The next few years continued at the same pace as those days following Lois' death; slow, plodding. Things were all right. He managed. He had the news on the tube and the guy next door, Joe, with whom he would go out for a beer once in a while, play cribbage or chess with, or mutter about life's pits with.

That is until Joe disappeared one day. There was no warning. He was just gone in the middle of the night, all belongings left behind. There was no family to contact, so Harry just notified the police. After a brief investigation, it was believed that Joe had taken off with his girlfriend, someone he'd been seeing over the previous two months, talked about enthusiastically, but neglected to introduce to Harry.

Since then, there had been nothing but his thoughts.

Jennifer was still smiling, waiting patiently for his answer. He took another quick glance to Melissa. She made him nervous, but the idea of an honest to goodness home cooked meal after all these years made his taste buds stand up and speak for themselves, "Yes, thank you, I will be glad to," quickly fell from his lips.

The next night, Jennifer, he found out, was a vegetarian, but she cooked in such a manner that Harry quickly forgot that he was not eating meat.

"We must keep the body clean, Harry," she started. "Consuming meats, be they red or white, will only make you slow and open to all sorts of maladies." She poured a glass of spring water. "And that includes what we drink."

"Jennifer," he started, after savoring another mouthful. "This is outstanding."

"I'm glad that you're enjoying it. I'm sure that it beats frozen this and frozen that or fast food. It must be welcome. Be sure to save some room for dessert."

The woman was a dream come true to a lonely man.

Melissa remained silent through the meal; the only sound she made was placing her fork back on the plate after taking one of her infrequent bites.

Still ever smiling when the meal was complete, Jennifer excused herself and started clearing the table. Harry stood to help, but gently placing a soft hand on his shoulder, she pushed him back down.

"You're our guest tonight. Enjoy being pampered."

Melissa silently rose to clear the table and assist her mother in the kitchen.

Immediately after the door to the kitchen swung closed behind them, Jennifer and Melissa started a conversation, most of which was muffled, but pieces bled through.

Jennifer: "No, not now."

Melissa said something indiscernible.

Plates went hard into the sink.

Jennifer: "Patience."

Jennifer led the way back through the door with three steaming cups of herbal tea; Melissa followed with a fruit salad.

The evening was finished off with quiet conversation around the dinner table; afterward Jennifer sent Harry home with a plate of leftovers and a promise to do this again.

As the next several weeks went by, the dinners became a regular happening and were quickly expanded to lunch and then healthy breakfasts, all delivered in a timely manner each day by mother and daughter.

Melissa seemed to be growing forlorn, paler, almost shrinking within her clothes. The girl was always by her mother's side. She never left it. Whether it was sitting with them at his kitchen table or casually walking around the complex, she was always there; arm ever intertwined with her mothers.

Then, about four weeks after the first dinner, in the middle of the night, Harry awoke - a sound, outside his window, so quiet he would not have heard it if he had not been tossing and turning through the hot steamy night.

He awoke with a start, sweat dampening his tee shirt. Wiping a shaking hand across his forehead, Harry became aware, again, of the sound. A click. A snapping twig? A turning of a doorknob? Even a full-grown man of sixty-five can imagine wild things in the dead of night.

"Who's there?" he called out.

Silence.

Despite that, he suddenly no longer felt alone.

Then, a rustle of the bushes outside the window.

"Who is it?" he called again.

Shadows from the trees outside his window wavered back and forth on the moon lit walls of his bedroom, beckoning him to come and see.

Snap!

He jumped.

Fool, he thought, you're sixty-five years old!

In the next moment the grownup Harry found no consolation in that false bravado, when from the side of the window he saw a figure slithering, as if poured from the boards of the building.

Moonlight illuminated the face.

Melissa.

Her powder blue nightgown clung to her body like she'd been caught in a downpour. She stood silently.

"Melissa, what are you doing here? Is there something wrong? Is your mother ok?" Harry asked, raising himself on his elbows.

He wanted to jump from the bed to help the girl, but he could not move any further. As if hands held his arms and legs in place, he felt weight against his bones.

Her eyes shimmering with blood-red veins that reached to the corners like spider webs smoldered with passion. Though it had been more than ten years since he'd experienced a sexual liaison, that look - the hot burning embers of wanting, deep in the black of the eyes, came back to him right then, in the eyes of an eighteen-year-old woman-child.

Through strands of unkempt hair, Melissa stared at him, licking her dry, cracked lips. She placed one hand on the pane of each window for support, and began undulating as if in the throes of orgasm. She rotated her hips and thrust them forward, gasps of breath accompanying each movement. Her hands squeaked against the glass leaving smears of brown in the wake of sliding hands.

Harry thought for a moment that she had been in trouble, perhaps out sleepwalking through one of the local swamps and had been hurt, her body racked with pain that he had mistaken for pleasure. He tried to move to help, but still could not. He could only watch helplessly as she slid down past the windowsill and away.

Finally free, he lunged from the bed and rushed, unsteadily, to the window. Pulling the screen from its hold, he grasped the handles and cranked the windows open wider; he leaned out over the edge. The humidity lay on his skin like a wet cloth.

Melissa was nowhere. There were no footprints in the earth indicating that anyone had even been there.

"Melissa?" he called out.

Only the chirps of crickets and the croaks of distant frogs answered.

Had it been a dream? He ran fingers over the outside of the window and pulled his hand away moist with the remnants of mud. He glanced across the moon-lit court to Jennifer's condominium.

Dark.

Asleep.

That's what you should be doing, he thought.

But of course, for the remainder of that night sleep was to be elusive.

Harry chose not to mention the previous night to Jennifer, afraid she would think him crazy and not want to see him again. He went on as if nothing had occurred.

Two weeks later, after dinner, they sat on her couch as usual, for some quiet conversation. The night was unusual, in that they were alone. No emaciated Melissa with her sad eyes and her unnatural white pallor, clinging to her mother, staring blankly - or perhaps seductively this time - at Harry. Jennifer explained that Melissa had simply chosen to be in her room that night. As if this were normal.

Jennifer did much of the talking, Harry just watched her as she spoke. Her voice was velvety, distant, and he found himself lost in its tone. He was content watching the way her lips moved as she spoke each word, the subtle change in her eyes, her occasional crooked grin, the way she used her hands.

Long slender fingers, perfectly manicured, curled in and out of her palm as she spoke, pointing here and there. She moved them delicately, exquisitely up to her throat, then to her forehead to easily brush aside a misguided hair and then lightly between her breasts as she spoke breathlessly.

Then, suddenly, seemingly to emphasize a point, she reached out and brushed her fingertips over the tops of his hands as they lay in his lap. It was a feathery touch, no more, sending a slight jolt through him. He wasn't sure that she was even aware of what she had done. He jumped just enough so he'd felt his involuntary movement, but not enough so she noticed.

My, God, Harry Kirkland, he thought at that moment, I believe that you're in love! That realization astounded him.

It had been the first time they'd touched since their introductory handshake six weeks earlier and he wanted desperately to reach out, clasp her dainty hands in his own and hold them there. He wanted to tell her that everything could be good for both of them, together. Like a time years before, on the floor of the Victorian kitchen, he felt as if he were outside his body, unable to speak.

Her eyes were liquid, the pupils like pools of dark water, the dim light of the room reflected in them like tiny sparks. Had she turned down the lights? When had she moved? He thought that he'd been looking at her the entire time, never shifting his eyes. Panic began to rise; he felt beads of sweat form on his forehead and trickle down his face. Something was not right.

Jennifer reached out and touched his hand once again. She must have seen his distress. But her touch wasn't meant for comfort. It was cold, hard. She held him fast, clasping his hands almost desperately into her own. He felt her nails break the skin.

Cold fear swallowed him like some hideous beast. From the corner of his eyes he saw movement at the far side of the room; a shadow within a shadow.

Slow.

Deliberate.

Very slowly, he shifted his gaze.

Another movement not so subtle this time.

A step forward by . . . something . . .

Out of the shadows, luminescent bones lurched forward like a crippled old woman. Falling into the dirty light of the room, translucent flesh clinging tightly to an emaciated frame, it grinned horribly at Harry through twisted, broken teeth.

It was the eyes that caught Harry's memory. He knew them. Dark circles enhanced the red glow that he'd seen before, because they were the same.

Melissa.

She stood in place for a moment, rocking back and forth on unsteady legs, her arms hanging limply by her sides like a skeleton in a science class. Her body, now hidden behind the folds and ripples of a dress, the right sleeve hung off the shoulder down by the elbow. She looked like a holocaust victim.

She drew steadily closer.

Again he was unable to move.

Jennifer rose from the couch as if she had floated. She met Melissa halfway across the room, placed her arm around her daughter, and helped the rest of the way, all the while smiling, ever smiling. Except this time, it was an evil smile - full of death.

When the two were directly in front of Harry, his feet touching Melissa's, Jennifer reached up to her daughter, placed her hands on the dress, and ripped it off in one quick motion; the shredded fabric floated to the ground by her feet.

An old shriveled carcass stood before him, full of liver spots, warts and loose skin. Harry wanted to close his eyes to the revulsion, but could not. His body, it seemed, was no longer his.

Both women turned their attentions to Harry. He felt himself being pulled and yanked, incapable of fending them off. In moments, he was sitting back on the couch, helplessly naked, the cold air of the room bathing his body in an unwanted blanket.

Melissa, or this thing that was Melissa, eyed him seductively; the orgasmic passion that he saw two weeks before was in her eyes again. She ran bony hands over her flaccid breasts and across protruding ribs.

God, Harry wanted to cry, to just babble like an idiot and beg them to stop so he could leave here. But they would not allow that. These *things* wanted him to have no dignity at all. As if to emphasize the point, Melissa reached down between his legs and stroked him - grinning madly, proudly.

Jennifer sat next to Harry, on the couch; her eyes, wide and passionate, like bloodstains on the sudden snow that was her flesh; her lips a pale blue, were slightly parted.

She reached out a long tapered hand with fingernails as blue as her lips to Melissa. She gently took the younger girl's arm just above the wrist and held it there reassuringly, as Melissa lowered herself down onto Harry.

Both women rolled their eyes back in passion, somehow sharing the moment together.

Outside, a car drove by, the headlights swept across the ceiling like spotlights; a dog barked, and another, in the distance, answered; a car door slammed; crickets chirped; frogs croaked - life as normal. Harry felt tears roll down his cheeks.

Eyes closed, Melissa settled onto him in an evil passion, biting her lower decaying lip, seemingly to stem a cry of joy. She rubbed her skeletal hands over her body; a mass of tangled hair swirled across her face as her joy became more frenzied.

The she pitched forward, gripping the couch on either side of his head, locking her icy lips on his. Despite the revulsion, Harry felt his body betraying him with building fluid.

Melissa whimpered as she grew out of control. She took him with new vigor, grinding her hips into his and when his warmth spilled into her, she pressed her lips tighter to Harry's, sucking the breath, the very life, from him.

His heartbeat like a drum, thumping loudly, echoing off the walls. It was all that he heard. He felt his eyes go dry; his palette grew pasty. His tongue felt thick. His breath became shallow as it passed from him into her, along with the last of his life-giving fluids.

Harry was beginning to float; no longer physically part of what was going on. A quiet tinkle grew in volume, weighing on him, until it became the sound of shattering glass. This went on and on, echoing into infinity, squeezing out all images until there was total darkness.

Finally, light broke through the shadows and he could see the world from which he'd passed. Although on the other side, he could still feel the women sucking on his soul, introducing him to a pain far deeper than he had ever experienced before.

He knew all sorts of things about them now. Born eons ago by other names, in another land, a land that long ago passed into history, he could now see them for what they really were. He could see through their artificial visage to their aged, dirty souls, shriveled from centuries of being alive. Sucking gleefully life's breath from their victims, taking their fluids, until each life was taken into their own bodies.

All of this came to Harry in that brief moment of the shattering glass. It not only filled his mind with knowledge that he did not want, it filled his immortal soul with fear. He thought he would have burst from all the pain and fear had he not suddenly seen another with him in this isolated place.

The figure, barely in Harry's vision, was wasting away. Sad. Lost. Dark circles around eyes that were distant. Harry knew him.

Joe. His beer drinking buddy now stood impassively. His skin, translucent, hung like a much too large shirt off his gaunt frame.

Harry could barely stand to look at his friend.

The shame and regret of that moment was brief, because in less than a breath, Joe was engulfed in a flame of blue that burned brightly, reaching upward, licking the cold air, like fingers pointing to God.

Joe's face became a twisted mask of anguish. He screamed silently. Then he was gone. The flame faded away into a wisp of smoke curling into the air, leaving no trace of anyone or anything.

Harry's pain was less now, though still constant. The vampires had turned their attention to new prey. Jennifer, now the one wasting away, her flesh like rubber, was clinging desperately to her companion. Melissa, younger, smiling, priming the next victim with cleansing foods and seductive charm, was stunningly beautiful, even more so than Jennifer had been. Auburn hair cascaded over her shoulders in waves. Her eyes, crystal blue, danced, mesmerizing the poor chosen soul. Her mouth full, her lips thick, and her laugh, playful and lilting. Like a song.

Their victim appeared as eager as Harry had been. As countless numbers before them no doubt had been. This is how *they* fed - on the desperation; the empty life that echoes with being alone and hating it, the lonely needing to be wanted.

Time passed ever so slowly, as if the clock of each day ticked over a period of days, sometimes months. Through it all Harry thought of the blue flame, knowing it waited for him. The thought brought both fear and longing. It would most surely be painful . . . yet it offered hope, hope of being free, eternally free. He prayed for its swiftness, prayed that it would send him to a better place.

When the moment came, Jennifer mounted her new life supply, and Harry found himself oddly giddy with anticipation. He watched as her eyes rolled to the back of her head, her skeletal hands groping her flaccid breasts, her soft abdomen, even her emaciated face, almost trying, it seemed, to tear the old flesh from her bones in order to make room for the new.

Then, the shattering glass resounded again and the new one passed into Harry's world, a shadow in the corner of his vision. Then the blue came. It came from within Harry, hot and painful, and he could hear what remained of his soul sizzle as it burned. The pain was far greater than anything he had ever imagined. Greater even than the soul-sucking vampires. Tears came and he could not stop them; one last indignity. Damn them to hell, he thought as the flames licked at him, consuming his ravaged spirit and devouring his soul.

***

The Scarlet Galleon

Mark Parker

ADRIFT – 1634 A.D., Somewhere off the Coast of Spain
The Orenta has been at sea for so many days, my crew has nearly
lost count. Days melt into nights, nights bleed back into days, until
sunlight, starlight, and moonlight together, have become one relentless
fabric of waning hope. Teasing us like an all-too-distant mirage.
Tempting the weak of heart, and causing even further suspicion, in the
minds of those seafaring souls who have lived long and hard enough - to
not be misled by the beguiling vixens that are the celestial bodies above.

Santos Consuega, Captain of the *Orenta,* had all but run
out of excuses to offer his men for all this maddening *drifting*
they'd been forced to endure. The war had not been kind to
the *Orenta.* Her sails had been irreparably damaged by round
after round of cannon fire, and her two main masts were
listing - much like the Captain's own flagging spirits. And, if
that wasn't enough, night was once again upon them.

In deep, velvety folds, the night air stood deft and
infernal around the *Orenta,* much like the abysmal
nothingness of Hell itself, had only the Fates been merciful

enough to deliver the vessel and her bereft crew to its obsidian shores.

But alas - as of yet - it had not.

Rather, Consuega and his men had been consigned to this earthly hell of supposition, knowing full well that land must be out there somewhere…perhaps neither close nor far…but surely within enough proximity to keep the Captain's mind from forever guessing of its whereabouts.

If only I could deliver the galleon and my crew to the hope of some distant shore by the fanciful endeavor of imagining it so.

In his despair, Consuega knew nothing could be further from the truth.

Even now he found himself wondering if he and his men would ever see land again. But then, as if in answer to his unarticulated question - not yet voiced to the entombed silence of the listless night around him - came a clamorous sound that all but tore the night in two. It was as if the stalwart crust of the earth itself had somehow risen up through countless fathoms to meet the vessel's sea-ravaged bow, just as the wayward warship's bulk came to a sudden and hull-shearing halt beneath Consuega's own uncertain footing.

The mind-rending thought was like a sulfurous thing; exploding and re-exploding in the Captain's mind until he was able to wrap the breadth of his well-schooled intellect around the enormity of the matter. The *Orenta - his* Orenta - had run aground under the blackened veil of night.

Once the sky-splitting cacophony of the vessel's grounding had subsided, all the creaks and growls gradually put to rest, there came a moment of the most unnerving silence, the likes of which Consuega had never before encountered. Such voluminous silence caused the Captain's already unsteady mind to question whether the grounding had occurred at all.

Despite the caustic heat of his surroundings, the air in Consuega's lungs had frozen. His mind was a jumble; thoughts colliding one into the other. He desperately fought to seize upon *anything* that might help stabilize his battle weary mind and reconnect him to at least some sort of rooted truth.

Try as he might, Consuega couldn't find a single thing to latch onto. Not one moment's worth of consolation to stave off his most disparaging of fears. There was no vestige of reprieve to glean strength from, nothing to rightly exorcise the thrashing tangle of demons that assaulted him from all sides; tearing at his weakened will with their most tortuous of tests.

The *Orenta's* grounding was a fate he and his crew would be forced to endure together, just as they had so much since first departing from their beloved Spain all those months ago.

Although the *Orenta* boasted a crew of a hundred men or more, Consuega had never felt more alone in his life. Such deafening silence threatened to undo him at any moment. A solitary soul adrift on a sea of malignant isolation; a man desperate to find his way home.

In the expanse of a single well-drawn breath, the Captain could feel the weight of his current predicament seated upon his chest, as if the *Orenta* itself had somehow been hoisted upon him - the weight threatening to crush the very life out of him where he stood.

The warship's waywardness had been dreadful enough, to be sure, but it was his orders alone that had caused the vessel to veer so completely off course, to encounter grounding as it had. With the supine expanse of blackened night draped over them like a moisture-laden funeral pall, it was as if they were already dead.

And, in many ways, they were!

Consuega's eyes fought hard to catch sight of more than just the *blackness* that surrounded them. But, absolute as it was, rather than start out in any direction, the Captain simply lowered himself onto the damp foredeck beneath him, and reluctantly began to weep.

When he felt as if the very life was about to slip from him, the Captain noticed a cluster of infinitesimal orbs; ruby lights dancing before his still watering eyes. Deft slices of air danced around his face with shifting urgency, as the fiery pinpricks of light grew ever near. He began to sense - rather than hear - a tonal squealing sound that lent an animal quality to the moment, lacing the ashen air with a kind of coexistent hope - and *terror*.

Within seconds of first noticing them, the orbs of ruby light that had been mere dots moments earlier - on some indistinct, indiscernible horizon - were suddenly all around him; followed by a terrible sensation that coursed up and down him, like nothing he had ever encountered before.

It was as if he was being lashed at from all sides by invisible reeds of tempered steel, slicing welts of agonizing pain through layer after layer of fabric, to the surface of his taut skin underneath. Whipping sounds flew up and down his huddled figure, then spiraled higher, up to the creaking masts that undoubtedly still loomed overhead, and the sluggishly flapping topsails, whose movement might be more conjuration than anything, given the tenuous state of the Captain's uncertain mind.

After a few moments, with an abruptness of force and ferocity, Consuega felt himself suddenly caught up by the ruffle of his shirt and brocaded collar of his heavy waistcoat, and unquestionably borne aloft - as if by some unseen winged creature - lifting him higher and higher, until he was certain he was situated at the very threshold of the heavens themselves.

With the brutal force of such maneuvering, the Captain both heard and felt the silken fabric of his shirt being torn away - as if by some meat starved creature come to feed. Then there was a terrific stabbing pain at his neck, slicing into him over and over again, just beneath the lobe of his right ear. A ghastly wash of heat enveloped him, and there was a sickening *sucking* sound that followed the pain; threatening to unravel what little sanity Consuega had left.

The searing pain was both bestial and bubonic - and *lasting* - which seemed all the worse by measure somehow. Still aloft, his body grew limp, then - sagging as it went - the Captain was falling...falling...falling...until he hit the deck of the *Orenta* with such blinding force, he most certainly must be dead, and had all but halved his beloved vessel in two, on his way down into the infernal depths of the netherworld.

With the coming light of dawn, Consuega was surprised to feel himself stir. Though his body was wracked with painful spasms, he grew to feel a sense of panic in realizing the fall he only *half* remembered, hadn't claimed his life as he might have suspected. In his sleep or unconsciousness, the blackened night had been replaced by a tenebrous cloud of weak light, giving renewed context to a world he both knew - and *didn't*.

Scanning the distant horizon from where he rested on the well-trodden planks of the vessel's aft-deck, Consuega took note of the fact that there was still no evidence of land in any direction. At least not from where he was currently situated, looking up at things from such an awkward angle as this.

On the side of the *Orenta* he could most readily discern, there were only mercurial swells several decks below, whispering a kind of *hissing* sound, each time they washed against the motionless hull of the grounded warship. As he attempted to shift his gaze to the lower deck where his men would normally muster, the Captain's heart sank at what he saw laid out before him.

In enormous, tilting piles, his crewmen were strewn about the deck like so many discarded human-sized rag dolls. Heaped - one upon the other - the mounds of men created an indeterminable mass of human carnage that was a clear and fitful reminder of how the Captain's own evening had played out.

He remembered the ruby orbs of light…the slashing sounds…the steel reeds lashing at his taut flesh…then the *rising* higher and higher…that terrific pain and terrible *sucking* noise…the animalistic squeals he heard before being let go…then that heady downward rush…crashing into the unyielding deck below…all played out mere moments before what he believed to be his own inevitable, if not untimely, death. Then *this!*

Despite the heavy clouds, the lazy heat of the morning sun took prominence, causing Consuega's stomach to lurch at the coppery scent of blood, and the unmistakable stench of loosened bowels. The admixture of odors was near paralyzing. He couldn't move himself from his current posture, so instead just laid there; permitting himself to take in what could only be described as the distorted landscape of a crude - and *cruel* - sort of dream.

Only this was no dream. Daylight after all, was quickly dawning.

And he was most assuredly *not* dead. In fact, it would seem, far from it!

From where he was situated, it looked to Consuega as though some treacherous gang of murderous cretins had overtaken his vessel during the hushed vestiges of night, and had slaughtered "en masse" his crew from bow to stern - not leaving a single soul alive, save himself.

The higher the sun rose in the hazy sky, the more profound became the miasma of blood, feces, and ensuing rot, that blanketed the silent decks of the *Orenta*. Thankfully no breeze stirred to lift the noxious stench to Consuega's nostrils with any sort of real fervor. The topsails still clung lifeless like withered serpents around the leaning twin masts, and the bulk of the *Orenta* still sat motionless beneath the captain's fallen frame.

His wounds from the previous evening grew painful once again, aching with renewed enthusiasm. Of course he had nothing chemical to stave off the swelling agony that filled his shattered limbs; not even a swig of rum for that matter. The tears at his neck stung afresh with the insinuation of salt and sun.

Giving into his understandable exhaustion, Consuega permitted his head to rest on the broad planks of the aft deck once more, where the evening's indescribable events had left him - and quickly drifted off into a kind of desperate slumber. Soon he was once again rolling from side to side atop a roiling sea, with the buffeting wind filling the *Orenta's* sails, heading him in the direction of his beloved Spain. A thought that warmed his heart better than any mouthful of spirits could. In dreams, his pain was gone; his crewmembers were alive; and things were once again under his watchful command. He was Captain of the *Orenta,* and his faithful men respected him; once again confident in following *him* - as well as his orders. Although war would most likely always be a part of their experience, nothing untoward would befall them again.

With the sun ever higher in the mid-morning sky, Consuega was awakened by the din of squeals that sounded much like those from the previous evening - but luckily weren't. Looking up to the grayish sky, Consuega saw a swirl of seagulls spiraling overhead. Awakened as he had been, to a state of apprehension, Consuega flew to his feet with little effort, and was surprised to feel himself more awake - and *alive* - than he had been, in quite some time. Though he could not have slept more than a few hours at most, not only did the Captain feel refreshed, but also had a more glaring perspective on the scene he'd only half taken in earlier, while sprawled out on the expanse of the aft deck. The scene of carnage was truly something to behold, and not - in the least - in any sort of good way! Perhaps in an effort to calm himself through ritual, he searched his pocket to retrieve his journal once more.

My felled crewmen are stacked atop one another, and it appears as if gallons of blood have been sprayed all over their corpses, giving the

*scene an all-too grotesque effect. What could any of it mean? And why
would anyone set so determinedly on this kind of destruction - leave me
behind; the only soul left to tell the gruesome details of such a string of
horrible events. Why?*

Taking several steps forward, the Captain heard
something he had not noticed earlier. From the tallest heap
of felled bodies, came a low and guttural moan - almost like
that of a growl - which clearly sounded more animal than
human, but didn't make much sense to his faltered
perception. Naturally kicking into protector mode, Consuega
flew across the aft deck with surprising ease.

When he drew closer to his slaughtered men, the Captain
was forced to take notice of something he couldn't really
begin to comprehend, let alone explain. Not with any
measure of bearing or truthful understanding.

On the death riddled faces of his men - many of whom
he'd come to call friend over the years they'd served in Queen
Isabella's Armada - Consuega noticed snarls deeply creasing
each man's face, in what he suspected was a fitful grimace
before dying. He also saw that each man's mouth was
bracketed with enormous fangs, much like those on the
ferocious Bengal tigers they'd seen in their travels; making
each one of his crewmembers appear more monster than
man in the faltering light from overhead.

Each face wore dark traces of blood-speckled gore,
much like the lashings he himself had encountered during the
blindsided onslaught the previous evening. The only thing
different about these men's appearance was that their
markings were beginning to smolder - as if lit by some
internal flame, fighting diligently to work its way out.

Wiping his sweat dampened brow with a tattered sleeve,
Consuega was aghast to note that each face his weary eyes
took in, smoldered as well, writhing with a bizarre kind of
ecstasy that, in his mind, didn't justifiably suit the occasion.
How could it, after all? Each one of his felled men was *dead*,
weren't they? Or at least he had thought them to be.

It was all a dizzying truth he didn't want to have to riddle out for himself; not now, or ever, for that matter. Such truths were ones he could well do without. It was all too much for his already weakened mind to comprehend. In this case, ignorance truly was bliss. And he was more than satisfied with that. After all, what would the alternative be?

As the morning sun began to burn with an intensified strength, the mounds of undulating corpses began to sputter, hiss, and pop, until the truly unthinkable began to occur. One by one, the *Orenta's* crewmembers began to stand up from where they'd been heaped on the lower deck, and walk around aimlessly in wide circles... moaning with every labored step.

Within seconds each *corpse* began to smolder, catch fire and then blaze with the ferocity of the sun itself, flames licking high into the weighted air above them, like the flickering tongues of a brood of hellish beasts.

Crashing into the varnished surfaces of the grounded warship, the roiling flames from the mass of burning corpses caused the *Orenta* to burn with a kind of unthinkable fervor. Looking down at his own swaying form, Consuega saw similar flashes of molten light beginning to flicker beneath the surface of his own smoldering flesh.

Along with his crew *and* vessel, the bereft Captain was being ravaged from the outside in. With a sudden wind whipping about, lifting the burning flames of their death higher and higher into the slowly shifting sky above, coiled by a noxious cloud of the blackest smoke, the *Orenta* and her crew were now glowing with a phosphorous intensity that, until now, was reserved for the abysmal works of distraught poets and writers of penny dreadfuls - and the frightfully delivered lines of brimstone sermons, harshly preached in the spiraling cathedrals of their blessed homeland.

With a final gasp of resolute terror, Consuega caught himself against the aft deck railing, before tumbling, along with his men, to their well-earned *deliverance*, in the now swelling sea below.   ***

Dangerous Dan Tucker: Vampire Gunslinger

Maynard Blackoak

The north Texas night found me perched wearily atop my faithful mustang, Mesquite. We had been riding since the break of dawn, headed for a range war just across the Red River, into the town of Cale, in Choctaw Nation. Fred Sterritt, the man who had hired my gun hand, awaited my arrival with a one hundred dollar payday for my services. It was to be a quick job, with only a rival rancher's young, inexperienced hired gun and a few slow handed cowhands that I would be facing.

Feeling Mesquite's lumbering gait, I knew my horse and I would need a decent rest before continuing on to Cale to meet with my latest employer. As we topped a hill in Dennison, overlooking the Red River, I spotted a cantina sitting on the Texas side of the river. I decided to pay the little establishment a visit, for a few drinks and a period of rest before continuing with my journey.

While my horse refreshed himself in the waters of the river, I ventured inside the lively confines of Rosarita's cantina. Strolling casually, I made my way through drunken cowboys and the saloon girls who coquettishly helped separate patrons from their money. Two of the ladies approached me, as I headed toward the bar. Not wishing to be relieved of my money, nor in the mood for their brand of company, I declined their offers.

After purchasing a cheap bottle of watered down whiskey, I searched for an empty table where I could enjoy my drink in solitude. Spotting a place in a corner, I navigated through the raucous crowd. Sidestepping stumbling cowboys and prancing saloon girls, I was vigilant to keep from bumping into anyone along the way.

The slightest wrong move on my part could instigate a fight that I wished to avoid. Not that I feared any man there. I knew that I could take any one of them if it came down to it. However, I lived by a strict code. I didn't believe in looking for trouble. But rest assured, I was ready with a gun if it found me. That code had kept me alive in a dangerous profession for many years, while most my contemporaries had met their ends long before.

As I neared the table, my eyes inadvertently made contact with the most alluring woman I had ever seen. Her eyes were like the blackest velvet, sprinkled with stardust that sparkled in the flickering candle light. Long, black hair flowed behind her like a train, gently rippling in the breeze. Her silky smooth, burnt umber skin wrapped her in beauty, enhancing her perfectly constructed features.

I was struck by the odd nature of her presence there. While most the women who worked saloons had a tendency to be hard and coarse in appearance, she seemed soft, almost demure. She carried herself elegantly, passing among the rowdy patrons and shamelessly flirtatious women.

"May I join you?" she inquired, after gracefully strolling up to my table.

"Nothin' personal, m'am. I'm just not lookin' to share right now. I just want to have a quiet drink alone." I refused, even though I could not take my eyes off her.

"I only want to sit and talk to you." she countered with a sly grin, "I have no interest in your drink."

Though I wanted to be alone, I found myself agreeing to her company. There was a mysterious hold her eyes had over me, something that not only prevented me from turning her away, but kept my own eyes fixated on hers. Never before had I encountered such mesmerizing beauty. The longer I stared into her sparkling pools of darkness, the more I felt myself drawn into a desire to be with her. I found the situation both vexing and at the same time, pleasing.

"I am Felina."

"Dan Tucker m'am."

"Dangerous Dan Tucker, the fastest gun in all the west?" she asked with a lilt of excitement in her voice.

I looked at her with a hint of surprise showing in my expression. I had not expected such a graceful lady to know of me and my reputation with a gun. Still, I have to admit it pleased me that she did.

"The one and the same." I replied, a twinge of vanity showing in my tone. "But I ain't so sure about being the fastest m'am. I ain't faced ever gunslinger out there. Truth be told, if I had my druthers, I'd just as soon not."

She nodded, chuckled amiably, then said, "Please Dangerous Dan, call me Felina."

"Alright Felina it is. And what's say we keep the Dangerous Dan talk under our hats. Don't want any of these yahoos gettin' ideas about makin' a name for themselves by takin' on ole Dangerous Dan Tucker."

"It will be our little secret....Dan"

We sat at that table for hours, mostly talking about my past exploits with a gun. It had been her turn to stare hypnotically at me when I recounted my experiences facing down a few of the most notorious gunslingers of the west. I could tell that she had been impressed by my adventures. Yet, I was caught off guard when she suggested that we take a walk outside, so we could be completely alone.

Passing among the river birch and cottonwood trees that lined the shore of the river, we walked without saying a word. Felina led the way, while I simply followed her lead, marveling at the manner in which the stars twinkled in her eyes. When we reached a tall, majestic oak, she stopped. Pulling my face to hers, she pressed her lips to mine.

Her kiss was like consuming the sweetest wine. I became light headed and dizzy. My body felt as if it were floating on air. All the pleasure sensors in my body stirred. If not for the fact that my thoughts were clear, I would have thought myself drunk from merely tasting her lips.

"Relax Dan. I want to give you a very special gift." she stated, stroking the side of my neck with her fingertips.

I stared into her black velvet eyes, responding "If I were any more relaxed Felina, I wouldn't be standing."

A hauntingly, pale hue came over her countenance, as if all the life had been drained from her body. Her eyes glossed over with an eerie haze. Even her movements seemed to flow in an ethereal manner. The netherworld image she cast, gave rise to a fear that none of my past experiences had ever given me. Still, I inexplicably found myself drawn to her more than before.

She began flicking her tongue across my throat. My body tingled with delight. Tossing back her head, she smiled wide, exposing her moistened, white teeth, glistening in the soft moon light. It was then that I got my first glimpse of those two, long fangs protruding from her mouth.

My mind wanted to flee. My feet, however, remained frozen to the ground. I watched helplessly, as she continued arousing the blood that coursed through my veins.

After placing a sultry kiss on my lips, she sank her fangs deep into the tender flesh of my neck. An instant of pain was quickly overtaken by a sensation of indescribable pleasure. My head swooned. My knees buckled. I felt my body straddling the precipice between life and death. Much to my surprise, I found it exceedingly pleasing.

Everything around me began spinning, then slowly fading to black. My senses overwhelmed, I couldn't decide if I felt fear or delight. I was struck by the irony of having survived countless gun battles, only to finally meet my end at the hands of a beautiful woman, if a woman she truly was.

I awoke with the sun rays filtering through the tree tops, flashing in my eyes. The sound of the flowing waters of the Red River filled my ears. Mesquite stood over me, his nose nudging my side, as he whinnied for me to arise. Though I felt a little woozy and feeling some pain from the puncture wounds in my neck, I was overjoyed and quite surprised to find myself very much alive.

Continuing on my way to Cale, I reflected on my chance encounter with Felina. I could not help but to wonder what manner of being she was. Over the course of my life, I had seen many bizarre things, and had met several strange people. However, none of my past experiences had approached my encounter with the lovely Felina and her spellbinding, caliginous, velvet eyes.

Sitting atop the galloping Mesquite, I pondered what, if any, aftereffects I would experience from her bite. Had she infected me with some type of disease that would manifest itself with a taste for blood? If so, would I become like her, preying upon humanity, just for a taste of the crimson that flowed in their veins? Or would it be that a raging pestilence coursed through my body, bringing with it a gruesome black death that would eat away at my flesh?

I arrived in Cale, a few hours before sunset. My employer, Fred Sterritt, emerged from his house, his expression showing a high level of annoyance.

"What the hell took you so long, Tucker?" he shouted in a huff. "You were supposed to be here two days ago."

His deportment created a stir of anger inside me. Employer or not, I was not accustomed to being spoken to in that manner. My hand began stroking the ivory handle of my Colt forty-five, as it rested in its holster. I took in a deep breath, and then exhaled.

"Sorry about that Mr. Sterritt. I met up with a little trouble at the Red River." I said, my voice composed, trying to smooth the tension of the moment.

"I'm here now, and ready to fix your problem." I added, hoping my readiness to get to work would calm his irate demeanor.

"Well then let's get to it, Tucker."

He mounted his horse. We rode north for several miles, until arriving at a pasture with a few hundred head of cattle milling about the rolling grasses. Approximately one hundred yards away, on the other side of the pasture, was a group of six men sitting atop their mounts. A short, pudgy man with a scowling face sat at the forefront. He was flanked by two others on each side, who looked to be cowhands. The sixth man hung back, as if trying to avoid being noticed.

"Okay Johnson. You ready for war or do you want to settle this peaceful like?" Sterritt shouted, as we began moving toward the six men.

"Nope. You're just going to have to find another place to water your herd, Sterritt." Johnson roared back. "This here's my land and my creek. If you want it, you're gonna have to take it."

"Just a warning to you. I got me Dangerous Dan Tucker here. All you got is some green kid and a few cowhands. Don't seem like much of a fair fight to me."

"The hell you say, Sterritt." Johnson responded with a grin, motioning for the sixth man to join him. "This ain't no green kid. This here's El Reno Jack."

The sixth man rode to the head of the pack, stopping at Johnson's side. Tipping his wide brimmed, black hat, a sprawling smile appeared on his lips, his silver teeth gleaming in the setting sun. On his hips were two, pearl handled, nickel plated Colts, each resting in elaborately ornate holsters.

I was very familiar with El Reno Jack's reputation. Like me, he had applied his trade for many years. Also like me, many dead men had been left in his wake. It was said that there were only five men in the entire west that possessed lightning quick reflexes and a deadly aim with a pistol, me and El Reno Jack being two of them. Men like us only survived a long time in our profession by not facing each other.

Sterritt glanced over at me, his face pallid with fear. "Honest Tucker. I had no idea he went out and got himself El Reno Jack."

"Well Sterritt, this changes things a might. A hunnerd just ain't gonna get it done. I cain't face the likes of El Reno Jack for less n say five hunnerd."

"You kill ever last one of them, and I'll give you a hundred a head." Sterritt countered, bringing his mount to a halt, as he decided that he had come close enough to the impending fray.

"Deal!" I accepted eagerly.

Sterritt turned, then rode off in the opposite direction, as I began approaching the six men I was to kill. I paid particularly close attention to my main adversary. Looking at the others, their demeanors suggested that they would allow El Reno Jack and me to face off first. When he began moving toward me, the others simply held their ground.

Riding out to meet in the middle of the pasture, we both presented a hard, confident façade to the other. We stopped with ten paces separating us, and then dismounted. Standing face to face, gun hands at the ready, we waited attentively for the other to make their move.

When his hand slipped toward his gun, I made my move. My hand was quick and my aim was true. My bullet pierced his chest a split second before he squeezed the trigger, causing his gun to shoot harmlessly into the ground.

I turned both my guns on the five men whose heads were worth one hundred dollars apiece to me. They returned fire, as they tried to scatter. But once again, my quick hands and deadly aim proved too much for my foes. One by one, they fell to the ground with my bullets lodged in their bodies.

Keeping my pistol drawn, I walked over to where El Reno Jack lay dead on the ground. As I stood over him, a shot rang out from the direction of where Sterritt sat watching. A sharp pain rifled through my side. Placing my hand at the spot, I felt the warm, moist flow of blood bubbling from my wound.

I sank to my knees, glaring in Sterritt's direction. He had double-crossed me. I had vanquished his enemies. But instead of paying me the money he owed, he had decided to give me a bullet. It was a betrayal I could not let pass.

Aiming my gun, I wanted only to repay his treachery with lead. However, my vision had begun fading to the point where I could no longer see anything, but blurry images. Death began overtaking me, as my strength began failing. Dropping my pistol, I crumpled to the ground with the world around me falling into darkness.

Sometime later, I awoke with the winds howling and rain splattering on my face. There was no pain, and no ill effects from the gunshot in my side. Placing my hand to the spot where a bullet had pierced my body, I felt no blood, nor any sign of a wound. I was unharmed, but didn't understand how.

I climbed to my feet, feeling stronger and filled with a new found vigor. My heightened senses detected sights, sounds and smells at a level of proficiency which I never before experienced. As I marveled over my enhanced self, I remembered Felina's words. She had wanted to give me a gift, and it seemed as if I had indeed been given one.

Testing my improved abilities, I drew my guns to test my reflexes. My hands moved in a blur, pulling my gun from its holster, aiming, and firing, all in less than the blink of an eye. Next I tested my vision. I found myself drawing, and hitting targets as small as a twig with pinpoint accuracy, from great distances. Before Sterritt had shot me, I had been a gunman of legendary prowess. Afterwards, I had awakened to find myself transformed into a gunman of supernatural ability.

I felt more confident than ever that no man would be able to get the drop on me. Even if by some miracle, someone did somehow manage to outdraw me; their bullets would do me little harm. The more I contemplated my future, the more I could not wait to exercise my greatly enhanced talents. Still, there was one lingering matter that needed to be settled between Fred Sterritt and myself before moving on to new opportunities.

Prowling stealthily, I skulked up to his house. Before killing him, I needed to know where he stashed his money. He owed for me a job completed, and I was determined to see that he fulfilled that financial obligation. Afterwards, I would repay his lead with some of my own.

Entering his house, I spotted a strong box sitting on the hearth. As I moved toward it, I heard the sound of a shotgun being cocked. Before I could turn to see who had me in their sights, there was a loud bang, followed by the smell of spent gun powder.

The shotgun pellets tore through my back in a scattered pattern. There was a burning sensation, as if my skin was on fire. After only a few moments, it stopped. I finished turning to see my attacker. I came face to face with a horrified Fred Sterritt fumbling with his shotgun, trying to reload it to empty its contents in my flesh again.

"You owe me six hunnerd dollars, you yella bastard." I growled at him, my face scowling menacingly. "After you ante up what you owe me, then we'll discuss the matter of your double-cross."

"It can't be........You....You're dead." Sterritt fumbled the words out of his mouth, his eyes widened with fear. "It just ain't possible."

I took pleasure in his fear. Tilting my head back, I released a gregarious laugh. The pale light of the moon filtering into the house, aided by numerous flashes of lightning, struck my face just so, giving Sterritt a good look into my black eyes, ashen face and glistening fangs. He recoiled in horror, backpedaling away from me. I slowly began stalking toward him, still taking delight in the look of terror in his face. He tripped and stumbled over furniture, trying to back away. I drew my pistols, squeezing their triggers. They clicked time after time, as each empty chamber made a pass into firing position.

"Now, unlock your damn strongbox….And I might let you live, you dirty som bitch." I commanded, once I had him cornered against a wall.

"Sure Mr. Tucker. Whatever you say Mr. Tucker." he acquiesced in an overly compliant tone.

He crawled over to the hearth, grabbing the strongbox. Fumbling through a ring of keys retrieved from his pocket, he nervously tried to find the one that would open the padlock that secured the box. With trembling hands, he anxiously fidgeted with key after key.

"Look here Sterritt. Get that damn thing opened and give me my money now….And if you're trying to pull another double-cross, I'll kill you right there."

My intimidation only served to increase his level of anxiety. His hands grew more unsteady, as he frantically kept trying to unlock his strongbox. I felt a twinge of sympathy for him, but only for a second or two, as the scent of his blood began to arouse a savage hunger in my gut.

Much to my surprise, I discovered that the more frightened he became the sweeter and more enticing the scent of his blood. It was taking every ounce of my will to refrain from tearing into his neck with my fangs.

"Do it Dan. Do not deny yourself the pleasure of tasting his fear." a familiar voice spoke from just inside the door.

I turned to see Felina standing in the doorway, her ethereal image set in an eerie glow by the frequent flashes of lightning that lit up the night sky. Surprised by her sudden appearance, my focus shifted from Sterritt. Seizing the opportunity, he darted away from the strongbox. Grabbing a wooden leg from a broken chair, he wielded it in a threatening manner.

"I read all about your kind in a book back east. You two just get outta my house before I shove this here table leg through your heart." he asserted, his voice sounding more confident than his expression showed.

Before I had a chance to respond, Felina was upon him in a flash. The table leg dislodged from his grasp, she had her fangs sunk deep into Sterritt's neck. The scent of his blood flowing sent my senses into a frenzy. Swiftly, I set upon him, savoring the crimson bounty that flowed into my ravenous mouth.

Just before the last beat of his heart, Felina pushed me away from him. "We drink until the brink of death, careful to never take in another's death. To drink of death would bring weakness back into our bodies."

"Okay Felina. Being new to this thing, I reckon I got lots to learn."

"That you do Dan. That you do. But you will learn quickly." she agreed, as she walked over to the strongbox.

She took the padlock in her hands, and then twisted it until it broke. The box opened, she placed a hand inside, retrieving a stack of currency. "We don't need keys to open locks. We take what we want, careful to never reveal the true nature of ourselves."

"This should sustain us for quite some time until another opportunity comes our way." she added, smiling deviously, as she fanned through the banded bills.

"Just one more thing Felina. How in hell did you find me?" I asked, my brow furrowed with curiosity. "I never told you where I was headed."

"I made you Dan. I will always be able to find you."

We left Cale as dawn began creeping over the horizon. From that moment forward, Dangerous Dan Tucker was dead to the world of the living, only to live on as a creature of the undead. My given name known only to myself and Felina, as we moved from place to place, applying my trade as a Vampire Gunfighter under many aliases.

***

Blood in the Water

Suzi M

The roar of the boat engine cut out, leaving only the slapping of waves against the sides of the craft. Lilith closed her eyes with relief and embraced the brief silence.

She could feel the eyes of the crew crawling over the back of her wetsuit and a cold smile lit her features for the briefest of moments until she remembered why she was on a boat a few miles off the coast of Rhode Island. She had business to attend and possible miles to go before she could enjoy any pleasure. She would wait.

"Ma'am?"

She acknowledged the ship's captain without taking her gaze off the surface of the water and mentally checked their position. If the notes had been correct, they were close to their target.

"We've reached the coordinates you gave us."

She tapped her long, red-lacquered nails against the boat's railing as she contemplated the ocean. It occurred to her that time had the uncanny ability to slip away unnoticed in a way that was akin to a one-night stand sneaking out of bed in the wee hours of the morning. Lilith contemplated her own lost time and sighed. Millennia had crept by unnoticed since she last considered ruling mankind and since she had tried to reunite her brethren. She had lost track of them, assumed they had all been killed in the Flood, until a writer in the 20th century gave her reason to believe they might be very much alive somewhere. With the blink of an eye she was back in the present moment and staring out at the sea, closing in on her goal.

She made a show of sniffing the air, but in reality she was opening herself up in a way that she had reserved only for one man over the years. Her eyes snapped open and she sucked in air. It was faint but it was there, beneath the waves. The stories had all been true and the writer she had tortured for the information all those years ago had not been lying. She glanced again at the long-dead writer's journal and gave a slow nod.

Turning back to the captain she said, "We need to go one more mile in that direction."

She pointed further out and the captain's expression shifted. "Why over there, if you don't mind my asking, ma'am?"

Lilith closed the distance between them and leaned in close. The tension she felt coming off the man was like an electric storm and it excited her. There was a pale mark shining on his left ring finger where he had pried off his wedding band as she had stepped onto the deck of his boat, and she knew she could have him if she wanted him. She drank in the energy that emanated from the entire crew like steam off of a cup of hot coffee and relaxed just a little. She was always a bitchy flirt when she was hungry. With effort she forced her fangs to stay put so her smile would not appear odd to the already skittish sailors.

"I *do* mind your asking, Captain. I chartered this boat for a reason, and it wasn't to get questioned."

"It's just, well," he glanced around them and lowered his voice, "Ma'am, there've been *stories* about that particular spot on the ocean you're pointing at. Some say it's cursed."

She angled her body so that it would block the curious glances of the crew and reached down, stroking the man through his pants. His eyes grew wide as he stared into the ice of her gaze, captive and helpless. She held him there, her voice low and soothing until he relaxed.

"Do this for me with no further questions, and I promise you won't regret it," she told him, releasing him so abruptly that he almost cried out.

The man nodded, dazed. It was clear there was something about Lilith that he should be afraid of, but it was equally clear at that moment he was in no shape to think logically or at all. It was imperative that he bring her to the place she had pointed out, and he had no idea why. He started the boat's engines and steered them toward the spot that Lilith had indicated, his eyes never straying from hers for too long as she watched him. The crew shifted uneasily as once more the engines fell silent and the boat rocked with the waves as they dropped anchor.

When she looked over the rail again, Lilith could feel the presence below the boat this time. She glanced to the gathered men and smiled.

"We're right over the spot indicated in my grandfather's journal," she said, "So let's get down there."

The captain approached her again, pulling her aside. His men looked nervous.

"Ma'am, if you go down there, you'll go alone."

She blinked at him in surprise. "What did you say?"

The captain looked uneasy as he scanned the faces of his crew. Each and every one of them was terrified now, and Lilith growled.

"What's the problem?" The anger seeping like venom into her words. "Is this a joke? Some way you make a little extra cash on the side, by taking your clients out and charging more when there's no choice but to pay?"

"No!" he exclaimed, "I – NO. We're not looking for more money. It's just this is a bad spot. I tried to tell you before…. We don't go here. *No one* does."

"Why the hell not?" Lilith asked him, annoyed.

The captain's tanned and wind-burned cheeks flushed with embarrassment. He ran a hand through his gray-flecked tousled hair and grimaced.

"Well?" Lilith asked.

"It's because of the Kraken," he mumbled without looking up at her.

She laughed and asked, "The *what*?"

"Kraken, ma'am. It's a —"

"I *know* what it is. I just can't believe in this day and age that there's a boat of chickenshits who still believes in mythological sea beasts," she said, her voice raised so that the entire crew could hear.

The flush that had started on the captain's cheeks spread to his entire crew at her words. It was partly the red of embarrassment and partly the blotchy purple of pure rage. Lilith's smile was cruel as she looked at each of the men, absorbing their anger, their shame, and their lust. Her gaze dared them to do something about their emotions as she pulled her long pale blonde hair back into a tight bun.

"I'm heading down there, boys. I'll see you in a few," she told them as the captain helped her fasten the oxygen tanks onto her back.

She looked around at the gathered faces and paused for effect. Not one member of the crew stepped up to her silent challenge.

She gave an irritated wave as she dropped off the deck of the boat and into the chilly Atlantic Ocean. When the bubbles cleared she made her way deeper into the murky water. The oxygen tanks had been mere formality. She didn't need them, and had to remind herself to blow bubbles every few seconds so the crew on the ship above wouldn't panic.

The crew. Lilith blew out bubbles of aggravation as she kicked her way through the water. She had hoped to have a human shield ready if things did not go according to plan. She had not anticipated that rumors of a Kraken would spook the entire crew into staying on the ship and force her to explore alone.

The deeper she went the darker her surroundings became until at last she closed her eyes and continued on sense alone. The hint of a beacon was stronger in the depths of the ocean, much stronger than it had been when she stood on the deck of the ship. She followed it blindly, her sense of her surroundings telling her when to change direction and when to stop and open her eyes. When at last she felt a pulse of recognition emanating from the deep she opened her eyes and switched on her flashlight.

She paddled backward almost instantly, unprepared for the sight before her. It appeared to be a large underwater pyramid at first glance, but she knew its true nature and that this was merely one corner of a much, much larger structure.

R'lyeh, she thought to herself with a grim smile. At long last.

There was a shift in the sand of the ocean floor beneath her as a doorway opened. She stared into the gaping darkness and descended into the opening, praying her long overdue visit would be a happy occasion.

Once inside the space beneath the sand, the doorway above her closed, sealing off the ocean. She dropped into a corridor without grace as the water ebbed. It was built high and wide, large enough to accommodate the passing of a horde.

She kicked off her fins and dropped the tanks and scuba mask to the floor with a clang. She winced, and waited to see if anyone would greet her. When she heard no noises other than the groaning of metal under strain far in the distance, she walked barefoot along the damp and chilly hallway.

The hollow silence of the place made her uneasy and she was glad her footfalls were silent as she moved through the dark, making her way toward the presence she felt deep within the structure. She reached a cavernous room and stopped to get her bearings. Corridors stretched from the large expanse in all different directions and Lilith was distinctly reminded of what a chaos symbol would look like if she were viewing the layout from above.

An odd slithering noise emanated from one of the hallways to her right, followed by more noises from the other hallways. Lilith held her breath and waited, praying that she had made the right decision.

What appeared to be albino snakes slithered into view from every hallway. They moved, faceless, into the great room. They lifted what might have been their heads in unison and seemed to sniff the air with absent noses before converging into a mass in the middle of the room.

Without realizing she had been doing it, Lilith backed toward the hallway from which she had entered. As she watched the snakelike creatures moving orgiastically over one another she prepared to run.

The creatures converged as they intertwined, building first one column of leg and then the second. Next came the torso, followed by arms and finally a head from which long tentacles squirmed blindly into the air. The tentacles paused suddenly and the head of the creature turned to face Lilith. It let out a low, wet growl, its face a mass of squirming flesh with holes where eyes might have been.

"Hi, Cthulhu," Lilith said weakly.

The creature made a noise that resembled laughter – if dead things in sewer grates could laugh. The stench surrounding the squirming flesh also suggested the presence of dead things in subterranean waterways and Lilith wrinkled her nose.

"Lilith," the creature said in way of greeting.

Its voice was garbled, and her name bubbled at what were its lips where the tentacles parted to smile. After a moment large liquid eyes filled the holes in its face, and blinked at Lilith as its flesh stopped moving. Muscle rippled beneath the slimy white skin as it took a step toward her.

"Why have you come here?" Cthulhu asked, the words more intelligible this time, though still wet.

"I have news," Lilith told Cthulhu with a sly grin.

"How long have I waited?"

She shifted uncomfortably and looked away. "It's been a while," she said, "And to be honest, you weren't exactly easy to find after the Flood."

Cthulhu took a second step toward her, "Did you search?"

"A little. Look, that's not the point here."

"What *is* your reason for searching me out, then?"

The distance between them closed rapidly with slow, wet steps and Lilith forced herself to remain calm. She put on a good show until Cthulhu was within arms' reach, towering over her tall frame by two feet. It was at that moment she realized the hallway through which she had entered the room had sealed off behind her.

She had rehearsed the speech she wanted to say so many times, only to freeze in panic and blurt the one name she knew would bring Cthulhu out of retirement.

"Enoch."

She meant to start with the outline of her plan for world domination, not automatically resort to dangling a man she knew to be completely innocent of any wrongdoing as bait. Well, it was out there now, so she had to follow through.

"What of Enoch?" asked the old god.

Up close Cthulhu was even more terrifying, with skin the white of fish bellies and a voice that would drive most humans mad. As they faced each other she could see things slithering beneath the surface of his skin.

Lilith took a deep, steadying breath and regretted it as the stench of rotting fish overtook her nostrils. She decided she could work world domination into the equation later, she would start by using Enoch to draw Cthulhu back to the surface. Baby steps.

"Let's talk about it on the way back," she tried, but Cthulhu grabbed her by the arm.

She stared down at the tentacles encircling her entire arm and fought the urge to run. The tentacles crawled over the fabric of the wet suit as if searching for entry. When they found none, they retracted back to finger length protrusions from Cthulhu's hand.

"We shall speak of it now," he said, "I have not lived as long as I have by exposing myself to the attention of beings who try to kill me." What passed for Cthulhu's eyes narrowed and he continued, "How did *you* escape the Flood?"

The tentacles tightened around Lilith's arm, once more stretching and expanding over the wet suit. Lilith watched with a sense of unease. She had seen them crush a man's skull with no effort at all. While she knew Cthulhu would not kill her, she was sure his sadistic tendencies were as great as her own and that he could make her suffer for a very, very long time.

"I know where Enoch is," she said at last, "But we'll need to leave here to get him."

The wall behind her opened and the hallway was once more accessible. She let out a small sigh of relief as she hurried down the passage. She paused to retrieve her scuba gear as both she and Cthulhu readied to enter the ocean.

"When we get close to the surface," Lilith told him, "Wait for my signal, okay? I brought a snack, but I'd like to have a little fun first."

Cthulhu shrugged and motioned for her to exit through the hatch and into the ocean water as it filled the hallway. She swam to the surface as fast as she could, hoping she would have enough time to enjoy herself before Cthulhu became impatient.

As she broke the surface of the water the ship's crew gave a cry of relief. They scrambled to help her back into the boat and she smiled gratefully at them.

She climbed to her feet on the deck and dropped the fins, tanks, and mask. With slow and deliberate movements she unzipped her wetsuit and peeled it from her body. The crew stopped in the middle of their tasks and stared at her.

"Gentlemen," Lilith said in a sultry tone, "You want me."

The gathered faces nodded at the command, drawing closer. Lilith stepped from the discarded wetsuit and held her arms out to the captain.

"You first," she said.

He nodded as he came to her. He was unable to resist her cold blue gaze and was glad she had taken the choice from him. The crew watched as she took her pleasure and fed upon their captain. No one protested when she threw the captain's body into the ocean, his blood coating her smile and the surface of the waves. She called across the water in a dead and dreaming language none of them understood. They were numb to their own terror when the creature joined them on the deck of the ship.

When the blood was finished flowing from the last member of the crew Lilith smiled at Cthulhu. Whatever her misgivings had been about reconnecting with the old one, her brother, she was glad she had. Fond memories played in her mind of past conquests and nights of bloodlust in a time when humans still feared the darkness because there were still things to fear hiding there.

Cthulhu watched her for a long moment, his white limbs stretched languidly over the skulls and bones of the picked clean carcasses of the ship's crew. There was not an ounce of flesh left on his piled throne, though the old god was still clothed in red spatterings from the blood of the men who had tried to resist their fate at the last minute. He ran a tentacle over his teeth and wondered at what point throughout the centuries of his absence human flesh had lost its gaminess.

"You did not coax me from my home for this, Lilith," he said quietly and his words mingled with the sounds of a rising storm blowing toward the boat.

He watched Lilith wipe excess blood from her face and body, her balance adjusted for the slant of the boat as his weight pushed the aft portion lower into the water. She turned her cold gaze to him.

"You know me too well," she said with a smile, "and you're right. I have a proposition that could be beneficial to both of us."

"I am listening."

"I had hoped to return us to our former glory in the pecking order, however it would seem my campaign is running out of steam. I'd like you to help me."

Cthulhu looked doubtful as he inspected a skull for any meat he may have missed. He poked a tentacle through the eye socket and swished around the brain cavity, but there was nothing left.

"How do *I* benefit from such a plan?" he asked finally.

"There are many cities now, all of them with underground tunnels and sewer lines. You can feast upon flesh once more and no one would have to know you were down there."

The old one contemplated the gathering storm clouds as they settled above the boat. He decided he would go along with Lilith's plan not for the potential new hunting grounds, but for the chance at revenge. He would leave the new hunting grounds to the others of his ilk.

"I have but one request for myself," he said.

"What's that?"

"I want Enoch."

Lilith shifted uncomfortably and wished she had not mentioned the name. In all of history, Enoch was the one human she respected and even liked. He had done what he could to help them, and had even tried to help their fathers during the original Fall. She was not about to let this one stipulation ruin her plan to return the vampires of the world back to their rightful place, however, and she would at last reveal to all of humanity what vampires truly were: Nephilim. Creatures of divine origin.

"Just Enoch?" she asked.

Cthulhu nodded.

"That can be arranged."

"Then you and I have a pact, sister."

Lilith hoisted the anchor and set the boat adrift as she climbed onto Cthulhu's powerful shoulders. The swim in the ocean had washed a good amount of his former stench away and Lilith smiled. Tentacles entwined around her naked flesh and held her close, reminding her of times long past as she settled into the familiar embrace.

"Where are we going?" Cthulhu asked.

Lilith pointed southwest, toward the shoreline. "That way. To a place called New York."

***

Vermilion

Bryan W. Alaspa

They say the town of Vermilion, Illinois is cursed. If you were to see what it has become, you might be willing to agree. Like so many things that happen around these parts, it goes back to a story about Native Americans.

The tale goes that the town of Vermilion was once on the fast track to becoming one of the biggest cities in the entire state. That much is known fact, as there was even a time when the city became the capital of the state of Illinois. Sitting high on the banks of the Mississippi River, Vermilion was a transportation hub for the steamboats of the time.

As my great-grandfather told it, there was a thriving community here and in that community lived a wealthy man who ran most of the town. He had a daughter, and that daughter was willful and wouldn't listen and she fell in love with a Native American fellow back in a time when Native Americans were still called things like Featherheads, Cochise and Injuns.

Needless to say, the father did not take too kindly to this and he forbade his daughter to ever see the "Scalper" again. Of course, like most of these tales go, she didn't listen. She and the boy went sneaking around and it was only a matter of time before the father confirmed his suspicions. He then paid some men to find the young Native American boy. And do you think he turned the boy over to the police claiming some false crime, or just ushered the kid out of town, threatening him never to return? No, he did neither.

The father had the young man beaten and then tied to a large log. The young man lay there, bleeding, arms outstretched like a familiar religious symbol, and the father pushed the log off into the rushing waters of the Mighty Miss. This is where the curse comes in.

Reportedly the Native American boy cursed the whole town of Vermilion, proclaiming the river would eventually swallow the wanna-be metropolis like a giant serpentine devil, wiping it from the face of the earth forever.

Whether or not there ever was a Native American boy, bound by love and killed by hate, no one knows for sure. But there certainly seems to be an air of doom around this place.

Vermilion did go on to become a thriving city, but there came a flood one day and most of the town was washed away. See, when the water receded a bit, it didn't recede the rest of the way, essentially turning the city into a small island in the middle of the Mississippi River. We are now a tiny township with rushing water on all sides, technically part of the state of Illinois, but with the only bridge taking us into Missouri.

So go figure.

The town has flooded several times since then. The Ole Miss is one mighty bitch when she wants to be. The last time I remember it being completely flooded was back in '93. The entire town was covered in something like nine feet of water. Those of us that were left, just about 30 people at that time, were evacuated. We all came back and many of us said we would stay here until the island was gone, but most of the young families that had been away on vacation moved away permanently, and several of the evacuees decided they'd had enough.

These days there are just fifteen of us, all of us descended from those founding families of long ago. There are a couple of young folks, but most of us are older, like me. Heck, I'm one of the younger of the older folks being only in my fifties. And the rest of the town looks like something out of a museum.

There's the downtown area with a small store and a restaurant that barely does any business. Thank goodness for the legend of the curse or we'd have no tourists at all. There's a few houses and there's even a park, complete with playground equipment, even though there are no kids to play on them anymore. There's also a small city hall with mostly empty offices, a library and a church at the far end, with mostly empty pews. It's a pretty town, with lots of trees and green grass, but it is also very quiet, with empty houses where there were once families. Quiet that is, except for the always constant rushing sound of the river when you're outside. People live in fear each spring when the rains come and wonder if this will be the year when the curse finally hits for the last time.

I awoke in absolute darkness the night the stranger came. The weather people had been predicting a bad storm all day. The year before, we'd had a drought in the area and people joked that maybe Vermilion was going to become part of Missouri and join the rest of civilization again. Then came the hard winter, with lots of bad snow storms, one after another after another and the town stayed buried in snow. Then came the rains that spring.

A worried and water-logged crowd gathered in the local diner, while Myrtle and Fred made their really delicious hamburgers and hand-cut fries. The rest of us gathered around and talked about the weather, debating the need to evacuate again.

"It's just a lot of nonsense," said Derek Brickson, the man who currently served as mayor. "They always say it's going to be worse than it really is."

"Yeah," said Alice Smithers, clutching her husband Wally's hand, "but we're due. It's been a long time since 1993."

"I say we stick it out," I said. "I think we'll have time to get across the bridge and get out of here if the rains are bad."

Outside the rain had stopped and the sun was now shining down. The sky was blue and it looked gorgeous. But these people had spent most of their lives living in Vermilion, like me, and we knew the next storm could be brewing just over the horizon At the same time, we had been here for generations, and to those of us who were still here, after the floods and famine and the other problems, it was a point of pride to stick it out. We wanted to be the last, but the last by being carried out to be buried, not the last because we all turned out the lights as we left. It may be hard for some to understand, but tradition, heritage, history meant something to us and just leaving seemed like defeat. It was abandoning our heritage and our history. That ain't something you can do lightly.

We all ate the burgers and talked back and forth, but like most of the meetings we had as a community, it didn't amount to much. The sun was shining now - it was just easier to go back home and watch the Weather Channel with growing anxiety than it was to actually start packing and moving.

When I went to bed, it had started raining again, but it was hardly a deluge. I even opened the window in my bedroom a bit because I liked the sound of the rain when I slept. It was soothing, not pounding and driving the way the sound of the river was. I was dozing when the first booms of thunder came.

I awoke suddenly, my eyes wide, staring around the room. It sounded like a trillion tiny ants, all of them wearing armor, stomping on the roof, walls, and windows of my house. My bedroom lit up in a flash and everything around me looked like a photo negative. This was followed instantly by a booming crash of thunder that shook the earth.

"Damn," I muttered.

I got out of bed and dressed quickly. When I made it to the living room I saw that the streets were already flooding. The rain was coming down in sheets. I hadn't seen rain like this even back in '93. I felt a stab of worry pierce my gut and I put on my raincoat and headed out. I got into my truck, started it wondering how much longer I could pretend this wasn't happening, turned on the headlights and pulled out slowly. Even with the wipers going full steam, it was nearly impossible to keep up with the rain. Each flash of lightning forking across the sky lit up the darkness. Vermilion was not a town filled with street lights, so it got dark at night. Each stab of lightning pierced the back of my eyeballs.

By the time I got to the parking lot of Fred and Myrtle's for the second time that day, it looked like everyone else had beat me there. That figured. I was notorious for being a heavy sleeper. Things had obviously gotten more serious. Amy and Clyde, one of the younger couples, had already packed up their belongings because their SUV was filled to overflowing. Several other cars were probably packed as well.

I stepped out in the pouring rain, which was now pounding Vermilion like a giant fist, and ran into the diner. The bell over the door sounded, startling everyone just as another blast of thunder rocked the ground and the building around us. I shook off my raincoat and hung it on a rack near the door. I tried on a smile.

"Well, who wants to call me wrong first?" I said as I made my way to the booth.

I got a few half-laughs out of that, but most everyone was grim.

"We were just discussing who was going to go up there and wake Martin," Derek said. "About to head to the bridge and get out of here. The weather service has officially issued a flood warning for this area and it looks like the rain ain't gonna stop for about twenty-four hours. We need to get out of here while we still can."

157

I nodded and then sighed. "Yeah, I guess you're right, Derek. We had better all head for the bridge before it's gone or they'll have to call in the National Guard."

Everyone sat quietly for a moment. The mention of the National Guard hadn't calmed any nerves. I wished that Myrtle had some coffee brewing, or maybe some of her great breakfast cooking. I loved her hashbrowns and that was not a euphemism. However, Fred and Myrtle had apparently locked up and were ready to go. As for me, I had a sister over in Missouri who would probably be expecting me and I had moved stuff over there years ago just in case these things happened. I kept thinking I might just move out of this place, move to the non-cursed land, but it was hard to leave the place where you grew up Even thinking that, it was still a tough pill to swallow.

Outside, the rain was still coming down like a waterfall and Derek took the lead. I was somewhere in the middle, behind Amy and Clyde. The rain was falling even harder than it had been earlier, if that was possible, and driving visibility was practically zero. I had a moment's worry that the river might already be rushing across the bridge.

We were heading toward the bridge, just out of the downtown area, when the sky to the west erupted in light. It was brighter than the lightning itself and the flash extended up over the trees and the houses. A second later the ground beneath us shook so hard that we all slammed on the brakes.

Derek got out of his car first. I was next. Then Wally Smithers came and Clyde followed. Derek was peering ahead into the rain, as if he could see anything. Derek took his job way more seriously than anyone who was mayor of a town of fifteen people should have.

"What *was* that?" Clyde asked.

"Was that lightning *hitting* something?" Wally was getting jumpy.

Derek shook his head. "No that wasn't lightning," he said. "That was louder and brighter than lightning and thunder."

"Then what was it?" I asked, now with a jagged knife of fear piercing me.

"I think something blew up," Derek said as if we hadn't all thought the same thing and looked back at us, squinting as the water ran into his eyes.

"What?" Fred exclaimed. "What the hell are you talkin' about Derek?"

"I'm telling you that I have seen dynamite used before and that sure as hell looked and felt a lot like dynamite," Derek said.

We all stood there getting soaked, staring at each other. The rain highlighted by the headlights of our cars, reminding us that we needed to move on. None of us seemed to know what to do.

"So, what blew up?" Amy said. All of us turned around in surprise. None of us heard her walk up.

"I don't know," Derek said, "but there isn't much up that way besides... the bridge."

All of us stared wide eyed now. "Who would blow up the bridge?" I asked.

"Derek, you are full of shit," Wally said, suddenly turning around and heading back toward his car. "I'm going."

"Wait a minute, Wally!" Derek yelled. Just then another boom of thunder hit.

Wally did not wait. He got into his car and drove around us. The water splashed us as the car flew past. I watched him go and wondered if I should head back home and hope this rain stopped, or drive after him. I mean, if someone was blowing things up with dynamite, how did we fight that? I certainly did not want to meet the man who was blowing things up in this rain storm. Flood or not, I was already thinking I wanted to be in my own bed instead of getting soaked while staring at my fellow townspeople.

"Well, let's go," Derek said and he headed back toward his car. With that, it was decided.

I got back into my truck and I turned up the heat. I was soaked to the bone and I was shivering. I had a feeling that the shivering was not because of the weather.

We made our way up to the bridge. When we got there, driving like a line of refugees from some movie. Wally's car was there, parked off to the side. It took me a moment to realize that Wally was standing there staring off into what was the Mississippi River, into the darkness where the bridge *should* have been. It was nearly pitch black and that should have been the first warning because the bridge was the one place normally lit up like Times Square, since we never wanted anyone coming home at night and driving off into the river.

I parked my truck and got out and I was beside Wally in seconds. I heard other doors opening and closing and feet sloshing through puddles. Our headlights shone out and it was obvious now that the bridge was gone. The river itself was angry and rushing past, but it was still below the flood stage. In other words, the bridge had not gone out because of the river.

"Who would do this?" Wally looked at me. I saw fear in his eyes.

"I have no idea," I said.

"Was everyone at the diner?" Derek asked. "Was anyone missing?"

"What are you implying?" I asked. "Jesus, Derek, you know everyone in this town. Do you think that suddenly one of our community was in a terrorist sleeper cell all this time? And what? They got the call to blow up a bridge in some town in Illinois that no one has ever heard about? For what purpose?"

Derek turned on me, the headlights making his eyes blaze. "Well, look at it, Martin! The bridge was blown the hell up! Someone had to do it. The bridge did not decide to commit suicide!"

"Both of you shut up," said Fred, who stood there in the downpour with his arm around Myrtle. "You know this means that someone either come into town and did this or someone on the other side did this to keep us here. We've got to get back to town now and call in the National Guard."

We all looked down at our shoes. I studied the puddle that was growing at my feet. I sighed. This had happened before, when I was much younger, and the Guard had sent helicopters and guys in boats to rescue people from their rooftops.

Suddenly, the earth shook again and a second later the rumbling roar of the explosion washed over us like a wave. It was so sudden and so loud that I opened my mouth and screamed. All of us turned and looked back the way we had come. It felt like judgment, like the end of the world. A huge column of flame and smoke shot up into the air. This was followed by another brilliant flash of light. We all felt the shockwave moments later. It was like getting hit in the chest with an invisible baseball bat.

"Jesus!" Derek yelled.

"Back in town!" Wally yelled, always stating the obvious.

"What the fuck is going on?" Amy screamed.

I began to run. I didn't want to stand around and stare at these people any longer. I bolted for the truck and climbed in. I saw the others running as well. Just as I got the car turned around, the horizon lit up again and there was more smoke. I could see that despite the rain, there were fires burning ahead. They wouldn't last long, but they were burning intensely right now and smoke was billowing.

We all drove far too recklessly back into town. The entire downtown area was ablaze. I pulled my truck off the road at the small park just west of the town square. The diner was an inferno. The church was devastated, the white steeple, a hallmark of the town, was gone. The city hall burned away. Debris was scattered in the street. The street itself looked as if it had buckled from the shockwaves. I stepped out into the rain again. Just like at the bridge I heard the other cars screeching to a halt behind me.

I felt fear. I felt true fear close around my heart . Smoke filled the air. The rain still pounded down, but there was apparently enough dry still inside those buildings to keep them burning. Maybe a gas line had burst. Whatever it was, the sky was lit with flames and smoke filled the streets obscuring much of the area.

"What is this?" Derek yelled, his voice becoming frantic, losing some of that authority he liked to throw around. He stood in the street with his hands by his side and his legs spread wide apart as if trying to make himself a wall, rooted to the ground. "Who did this?"

Wally was carrying the gun he kept inside the glove compartment of his car. We formed a kind of loose circle in the middle of the main downtown intersection. The city square, and the park, stood behind us, making me feeling very open and vulnerable.

"What do we do, Derek?" Wally asked. "Jesus Christ, what the fuck do we do?"

"What's that?" I asked, pointing into the smoke that was pouring out of the ruins of the diner.

"That's what's left of my goddamn diner!" Fred said, the pain in his voice agonizing.

"No! *In* the smoke!" I pointed emphatically.

Between the rain and the smoke and the darkness, I thought my eyes were playing tricks on me. Then the smoke became more solid. No. It was a shadow. The absolute absence of light, moving *through* the smoke and fire.

He came down the middle of Main Street like he owned the road. Like he had no fear. He was huge, a hulk of man, who as he walked continued to absorb the light. The smoke parted in his wake and he came towards us. As he came closer, his features, his clothes, gradually came into focus.

He wore a long black coat, like a duster. It hung across his massive shoulders and down to his ankles. The duster whipped like something alive around his legs. He wore a large wide-brimmed hat, hiding most of his face. His boots clacked heavily against the pavement. Looking like a gunslinger, his hands covered in black gloves, fingers spread, like they were ready to grab invisible guns hung low on his hips. Around his shoulder was a bag of some sort and I could see that it bulged with more bundles of dynamite.

"Hold it!" Wally raised his pistol. "Hold it right there you son of a bitch! I will shoot!"

The man stopped. I looked to my left and saw that Derek was as wide-eyed and terrified as me. No one moved.

His head held low, the stranger remained so still he might as well have been a statue. Then he slowly raised his head. The light from the fires and our headlights caught his face and I gasped.

His face was smooth and pale. He appeared very young, but gave off a feeling of a creature that was older, perhaps, than time itself. He looked at us with eyes that were beyond dark. They were black holes, absorbing the light around us, while simultaneously piercing us with cold. He looked from one to the other, taking each of us in. Marking us. His lips were a bruised purple, like a corpse. I could also see tufts of white hair poking out from beneath his black hat. When he was done looking at us he smiled at us with even white teeth from behind cold gray lips.

"Then shoot." His voice was not deep or loud, but I could feel it in my bones.

Wally fired. He did not hesitate. He was not a great shot but he was close enough to empty the pistol into the man's bread basket. When the six shots were done Wally kept pulling the trigger.

The bullets vanished into the dark folds of the long black coat. When Wally finally gave up, he raised his head and looked at the man. I saw Wally's knees go weak.

"It is judgment day," the stranger said. His voice not angry or filled with emotion. It was a statement, like saying that it was raining. "Judgment day for Vermilion."

And just like that the stranger moved. One moment he was there talking and the next he was in front of Wally. He was a blur that my eye just did not register. In a flash, he

163

reached into his coat, brought out a blade, and had slashed Wally's throat all in a matter of half a second.

Wally made a gurgling sound and then he started to falter. The stranger caught him and then pulled the spouting neck to his lips. As I watched in growing horror, the stranger began to drink the spurting fluid that jetted from Wally's neck. Despite the rain, I could distinctly hear the sound of the blood that dribbled down his chin and spattered onto the pavement. The gore flooded into the man's mouth and Wally got paler and paler, finally collapsing into the man's arms, his eyes rolled back into his head.

In shock, we stood there and watched as this creature drank Wally dry and then threw his empty corpse aside, and then turned its dark eyes toward the rest of us.

Derek tried to run first. He managed to turn and make three steps towards his car before the creature was upon him. There was a soft tearing sound, like a harsh whisper, and a blade was slashed across Derek's throat. Derek staggered away, his hands clutching at his jetting artery. Again, the stranger buried his face in the spray of blood, opening his mouth to catch as much of it as he could.

The others tried to run, but they never stood a chance. He got Fred just as he reached his car, his hands clutching the air and reaching for Myrtle who sat in the car staring as the stranger ripped Fred's head clean off his body and drank the blood that spewed forth. Myrtle was next - the man punched his hands straight through the window and ripped her windpipe out with his bare hands.

Amy and Clyde were running hand in hand down the street when the stranger descended upon them. His blades severed their hands and then slashed left and then right. More blood jetted into the rain and the stranger drank what he could before moving on. He moved like a blur, from person to person, slashing, cutting, tearing.

And I stood there in the middle of the intersection, unable to move. Each of my friends, people I had known for years, were torn apart in front of me, and I could not run. I could not scream. I saw judgment and it was coming for me last. Coming for each of the descendants of those who had created this town.

He held Amy's head by the hair in his right hand as he walked towards me. I knew that I should at least try to run, but it seemed pointless. I just watched as he walked up the road in the rain, the duster moving gracefully around his legs.

As he got closer, I could smell him. I smelled the fresh blood, but there was something else there, older, more ancient than anything man had made. The stench of a thousand years came off of him. Beneath that was the smell of earth, the dirt of millenia. Beyond that was decay, like rotting flesh.

He towered over me, blocking my view of everything save for the long black duster and the wide-brimmed hat. His old-young face, now blood-spattered, stared at me with nothing resembling hatred or anger. This was what he did. I knew it now. This was what he had always done, for centuries. Whatever made him what he was, this was now his task. He brought judgment - and judgment had come to Vermilion. His empty eyes, sockets rather than irises and eyeballs, regarded me. He cocked his head to one side.

"Do you not fear me?" He asked.

I nodded. "Yes. But would it do me any good to run?"

He laughed. Again, the laugh was not evil, not terrifying, but almost pleasant. "No."

"Why now?" I asked. "This town was cursed so long ago. Why now?"

He seemed to think about that for a moment. Then he shrugged. "It just is. You are the last of the descendants. It had to be now before this town vanished, as you all did as well. Then again, maybe the fates are just pissed off enough now and want this job off the books. For some things, there are no answers and, really, would any answer satisfy you?"

I nodded. "I guess not."

I felt like I should ask more. Here was a timeless being, the stuff of nightmares, the vampire out of the horror movies, who had probably seen things I couldn't imagine. Yet, I found I had no questions to ask. He had nothing else to say.

He moved in closer.

Judgment had come to Vermilion and it would finish by drinking my blood. Then the waters would come and finally wash the town, and its ghosts, away. Who was I to try and deny that?

I barely saw the blade.

***

My Boss is a Vampire

Michael David Matula

"Well, Ms. Bailor, do you have any prior experience as a personal assistant? Bartholomew Gannen expects a certain level of professionalism and know-how out of his employees."

Cameron Bailor shrugged, the warm Louisiana air feeling stale in the mansion's extravagant drawing room. The whole place smelled of dust and antiques; almost like the mansion had hardly been lived in over the past century or two.

Mr. Haberson noticed her eyes wander down to the bandage plastered to his neck, half covered by the collar of his gray mock turtleneck. Strangely, the bandage looked like it had been applied by a seven-year-old in the midst of a coughing fit.

Two rather distressing splotches of red had seeped through the gauze, and were starting to bleed into the fabric of his shirt.

Clearing his throat, Haberson shifted his backside in the premium leather of the lounge chair, angling his torso so his injury would be less noticeable.

"Not exactly," Cameron replied, her eyes skipping back up to his face now that the seeping neck wound was hidden from view. After looking at his sallow, droopy cheeks for a few seconds, she found herself starting to miss the neck wound. "I can make a mean cup of coffee, though. The kids I used to babysit for would absolutely *rave* about my cappuccinos."

A frown drew his hangdog features even lower, looking like he'd just tasted something sour. "I see."

It took all of her restraint not to face-palm, as she could almost feel her ice-breaker falling flat and shattering the surface of the lake.

Why did she say that? Why did she even attempt to crack a joke? She wasn't funny, not in the slightest. She was the last person who should be cracking wise in the middle of a harrowing job interview.

Cameron could see him judging her in his bloodshot little eyes. She couldn't say she hadn't been judging him from the moment she walked in the door, but still, it never felt particularly good to be on the receiving end of such withering contempt.

Should she tell him it was an attempt at humor? That she wasn't actually a caffeine pusher for toddlers? Or would that be an insult to his intelligence? Perhaps he knew it was a joke, and he was simply judging Cameron for her poor comedic timing.

"Do you mind if I ask..." she started to say, hoping to switch his mind off of her own shortcomings as a comedian and onto something he'd prefer thinking about.

Namely, himself. Men loved talking about themselves. If there was one thing she knew about men, that was it.

Except for when they had something to hide, of course.

"...what happened to your neck?" she finished asking, realizing the folly of her ways the moment the lead-laced words had fallen onto what remained of the proverbial ice.

She couldn't help but wince at his complete lack of an expression.

"I'd rather not talk about it," he grunted.

Of course he didn't want to talk about it. It was the one thing he'd been hoping she wouldn't notice. Why couldn't she have asked him about the weather or something equally bland and unalienating? Why couldn't she have complimented him on his fashion sense? No, that might have actually made him like her.

After all, he probably injured himself in some sort of kinky asphyxiation thing, and no one wanted to discuss their deviant sexual practices with a total stranger. Much less a pushy twenty-six-year-old who seemed to be unable to keep her mouth shut.

Mr. Haberson sighed. "Ms. Bailor, I'm sure you know that Bartholomew Gannen is a very important man. He may have retired from the limelight, but he still requires a capable, sturdy individual to fend off negative press and overeager fans. He needs someone who is willing to work long daytime hours, and someone who doesn't mind getting their hands dirty. Do you really think you would be capable of handling these responsibilities?"

Cameron tried to pull herself together. He was still talking to her. That was a good sign, wasn't it? At least he hadn't grabbed her by the scruff of the neck and tossed her sorry derriere out onto the regal front porch of the mansion.

She still had a fighting chance. And she still had four full "release-in-case-of-emergency" buttons to go through on the blouse. She had undone the first one in the car. She'd wanted that casual look.

The second button would show that she could be playful. She wasn't desperate enough to release button number two yet, but she was getting there.

If she undid button number three, it would show that she could be saucy. A real firecracker. A fourth button would cross the line into epic levels of inappropriateness. But she might still get the job.

She'd never had to go four full buttons before. She knew the day would have to come eventually, though.

"Absolutely." Cameron's mousy voice did its best to sound confident.

"Interesting."

Interesting?

"I must admit, Ms. Bailor," Mr. Haberson continued, "that I'm somewhat short on time this afternoon. Today was the only day I could interview replacements for my job in person, for I'll be unable to work days following tonight."

"Um-hm." There you go, Cam. Smile and nod. Keep eye contact. Don't look at the gross sex bandage...

All right. Well, don't look at it again.

"It saddens me to say," he told her with substantial hesitation, "that you've got the job, Ms. Bailor."

Cameron flashed her best "deer in the face of blinding headlights" look.

"Really? This isn't some sort of joke, is it?"

"It saddens me to say," he added, with just as much hesitation as before, "that it is not. We haven't had many applicants for the position, and I find myself unable to wait for anyone else. If Mr. Gannen is not satisfied with your work, then he'll deal with you later." Haberson cleared his throat. "He'll hire someone later, I should say."

"Sure."

She actually got the job? Seriously? With only one button undone?

She must be better at this whole interview thing than she thought.

Mr. Haberson knitted his fingers together. "I must insist that you begin working immediately, however, as there is much you need to do, and I have limited time before the dawn arrives on the morrow." He inclined his head toward the rather fusty coffee table to his left. "Your job responsibilities have been printed on the parchment there. Mr. Gannen has been somewhat... quiet, shall we say, over the last few days, so I took an educated guess at what some of his needs would be. If you require anything, try my mobile phone. The number's at the top of the page. My flight's at three o'clock this afternoon, though, so you may have some difficulty reaching me after that."

So, two and a half hours from now. Well, that should give her enough time to look over
the list and see if she...

"It's settled, then." Haberson unfurled his fingers and rose to his feet, extending his right hand toward Cameron. "Welcome aboard, Ms. Bailor. Do strive to do your best, whatever that amounts to in your particular case, as Mr. Gannen is rather quick to do away with incompetents."

She accepted his hand, too giddy about the fact she just got the job to concern herself with the heavy-handed dose of condescension.

He grunted daintily as he lifted up his suitcase, then started to power walk through the mansion toward the entrance hall.

"You're leaving already?" she asked his rapidly retreating form.

"You know how the rat race can get," he called back to her as the door creaked open. "Busy busy busy."

The door slammed shut behind him.

She waited to hear the tires squeal as he raced away in madcap cartoon fashion, but the walls and blacked-out windows of the mansion were much too thick to allow for it.

With him gone, Cameron finally allowed herself to take her first real gander around the place. She hadn't wanted to look like she was casing the joint in front of Haberson before.

As antiquated as it was, the mansion was still quite impressive, absolutely dripping with Southern charm and class. Aside from Mr. Gannen's apparent love of doilies, that was, as it looked like he had allowed his great grandmother to decorate the place.

"You've finally made it, Cam," she said, talking to herself and referring to herself by name, which was by no means the mark of a crazy person. "Actual, honest-to-goodness employment. A career, if I can keep from screwing things up like I normally do."

No more selling electronics of varying legality out of the trunk of her car.

Nope, she was in an actual building this time. A mansion. The kind of house that little houses wished they could be when they grew up.

"Personal assistant," she said. Again, to herself. Again, not crazy. "Has a nice ring to it."

Cameron sighed contentedly, straightened her blouse, then skipped over to the coffee table and plopped her backside down on the rather stiff and uncomfortable sofa.

This was a big opportunity. The chance to work for Bartholomew Gannen himself - a local New Orleans boy turned self-made millionaire turned quasi-celebrity turned paranoid recluse - was far too good to pass up. Or rather, the pay check was far too good to pass up. She hadn't actually heard of this Gannen guy until this morning, when she came across his job listing online and subsequently ran his name through a search engine.

But he was Rich. Notice the capital "R."

And charitable. Not with a capital "C," but still respectable.

Which meant he liked giving away money and wasn't some sort of skinflint. Which meant *cha-ching* for anybody working for him.

Which meant Cameron no longer had to worry about this soul-sucking dream she'd had of scraping together a living as a writer in an age where print was dead.

So long as she didn't screw this job up. Not that she had a habit of doing that, or anything. It was almost always never her fault.

The telephone burst to life, its ring stabbing into her ears like a purse-sized dog's overcompensatory bark.

She plucked the wireless phone up from the coffee table and held the receiver up to her ear.

"Good afternoon," Cameron said, trying to don her most professional of voices. "Mr. Gannen's residence."

"Yes," the man on the other end of the phone said, his deep voice as slow as dripping molasses, "it is. But I don't know you, do I?"

"Pardon?"

"You're in my house." The man's voice sounded utterly calm, despite the suspicion weighing it down. "What are you doing in my house?"

"Oh, um, hello there, Bar - Mr. Gannen, sir," she said, flustered, her eyes flashing from corner to corner of the drawing room, scanning the ceiling and shadows and doilies for cameras. For some reason, she felt like someone was watching her. Not a really new feeling for someone who still believed in ghosts, but unsettling nonetheless. "This is, um, your new personal assistant, Cam-"

"What happened to Victor?"

"Victor?"

"Haberson. Where did the dried up bag of bones flit off to?"

"Oh," she said, nodding, "the dried up bag of bones. Right. He just hired me as his replacement a minute ago, sir. My name's Cameron Bailor. I, uh, I assumed you already knew he was leaving..."

"'His replacement.'" Gannen snorted. "So he finally quit, did he? I guess I should be surprised he lasted as long as he did here. Never did have the stones for it."

"Uh..." she trailed off, not sure what to say.

"Fine," Gannen said, obviously charmed by her rakish wit. "You'll do, I suppose. The job's not complicated. Just do everything you're asked to, don't bother me with tiresome questions, and make certain no one, including yourself, wanders into the upstairs bedrooms during the day. I'm very protective of my sleep."

Sleep? During the day?

Weird.

But then again, he was filthy rich. And would soon be paying Cameron's salary. So he was entitled to a certain modicum of weirdness.

"I look forward to working with you - Cameron, was it? I'm sure we'll find it mutually satisfactory. See you tonight."

The line went silent following a gentle click.

Cameron hung up the phone, frowning while she attempted to work out whether she found him sexy or creepy. She wasn't entirely sure. Perhaps a bit of both. That was normally the kind of guy she seemed to go for.

Not that she would go for him. He was her boss now, and she fully intended to keep things professional. She wanted to try to avoid what happened with her last employer, if at all possible.

She already had the job, so her top button could stay open, but it wasn't going to be joined by any of its filthy little lower-button friends. No flirting with the man in charge. She was serious about it this time.

"All righty, let's see what we have here," she said, rolling up her sleeves to prove she was getting down to business, before she snatched up the bulleted list of instructions Haberson had left behind.

"First things first. I need to respond to a phone call from some reporter named Phillip Molloy. And 'keep him from nosing around the premises.' Hmm. Okaaay. Sounds easy enough, I guess. Phone calls are totally doable." She read the next item on the list. "Second, 'clean all of the red wine stains out of the carpeting in the reading room.'"

Wait…Cleaning? Really? Stain removal sounded more like a maid's role, not the responsibility of someone with a highfalutin title like "personal assistant."

Sighing, she returned her gaze to the list and continued reading.

"Third. 'Call Pauline DuBois and confirm her plans with Mr. Gannen for Tuesday evening.' No problems there. Fourth, 'confirm plans with Tammy Notaveno for Friday.'"

So...Ix-nay on the rue-love-tray, then. She couldn't say she had any intentions of being part of a romantic conga line.

"Five, deliver the dry cleaning to the cleaners. Easy peasy. And last but not least, numero six. 'Contact Sylvester Burke and make him understand the importance of confirming Mr. Gannen's alibi for the night of Saturday, the thirty-first of April. They were bowling. Remind him of that.'"

Wait. What?

"Alibi?"

Well, at least that meant he was innocent, right? Especially if he had someone who could confirm his story.

Innocent until proven guilty, and all...

She set the piece of paper back down on the table and rolled her eyes.

If this guy turned out to be some sort of psycho killer, she was going to be really, really disappointed. She had gotten her hopes up and everything.

That would be just her luck, though, wouldn't it?

This was the dream job she'd never known she'd wanted before this morning. She needed this job. It would really suck for her if this guy happened to have killed a bunch of other people.

She had to wonder, sometimes. Did the universe hate everyone equally, or did it just have it out for her in particular?

Maybe she was cursed.

After all, there was that time a few years back, when she was looking after little Paulie Jorgen. She did happen to stumble upon him stabbing the leftover Thanksgiving turkey with a grapefruit knife while reciting a voodoo ritual he'd learned over the internet.

She'd always just assumed that real voodoo deities wouldn't acknowledge the curse since leftovers were sacrificed in lieu of livelier fare, but maybe she was wrong.

Maybe all this time she had been fooling herself. Maybe the curse of the turkey really was hanging around her neck, causing her to mess up all of these jobs through absolutely no fault

of her own.

Because it wasn't like she could pinpoint *exactly* where she'd screwed up in all of the dozens of jobs she'd had over the years.

It had to be the voodoo. She was pretty sure she believed in voodoo. She believed in ghosts, after all. Voodoo couldn't be too far a leap away.

Cameron shrugged and lifted up the wireless phone.

Oh, well. No point crying over milk that hadn't even been spilled yet. There would be plenty of time for depression to set in tomorrow, should this dream job turn into some ghastly Southern Gothic horror movie. But for now, she had to get to work.

She lazily tapped Ms. Pauline DuBois' number into the back-lit keypad with her thumbs.

A phone suddenly chirped upstairs.

Cameron started to rise from the couch, intent on answering the telephone, when she recalled her new employer's policy regarding unscheduled visits to the upstairs bedrooms. So much for that idea. The calories she would have burned hoofing it up those steps would have to stay right where they were.

Returning to her spot on the couch, she waited patiently for Pauline to pick up. The phone continued chirping upstairs, coinciding perfectly with the ringing on the other end of the receiver Cameron clutched to her ear.

After the tenth ring or so, she ended the call with a tap of a thumb. The insistent phone upstairs instantly fell silent.

Oh, bother.

Pauline must have left her cell phone in Mr. Gannen's house when last she visited. Well, at least Cameron wasn't going to be blamed for it. This was Haberson's fault, if it was anybody's. He gave Cam the number to dial, after all.

Her scapegoat already chosen, she mentally crossed Pauline off the list and moved on down to the next lady in line, a Ms. Tammy Notaveno.

Cameron's thumbs went back to work, tapping out the digits in Tammy's telephone number.

A boisterous tropical ditty piped up in the kitchen.

"How strange," Cameron mused in her best musing voice.

Tammy forgot her phone in the house, too? It seemed unlikely, but perhaps Mr. Gannen liked his ladies unusually forgetful.

Cameron got up from the couch, phone firmly in hand, and followed the sound of the tropical music into the kitchen, humming along with it as she did. Upon entering, she spied a bulging black garbage bag slumped against the kitchen counter.

The ringing seemed to be emerging from within the belly of the bag.

"These people really do have a lot of money," Cameron told the garbage bag, shaking her head as she ended the call. "They're just tossing phones around left and right."

She wished she was rich. She wanted to be able to throw phones around with wild abandon just as much as the next girl.

The doorbell produced a resounding cling-clong noise. Cameron flinched, nearly dropping the wireless phone.

They had company? Who could it possibly be? The nosy reporter guy? The forgetful Pauline or her love triangle rival, Tropical Tammy? Someone else, out to get a piece of the infamous Bartholomew Gannen? A fan, perhaps? A fellow celebrity, interested in complaining about the high cost of fame, and how no one else really got what filthy rich celebs were forced to go through?

This was so exciting. She was in the house of a famous guy! People other than her actually knew who Gannen was. Even famous people! If she hung around him long enough, maybe she would become famous, too, at least locally. That seemed entirely possible, now that she thought about it.

She sashayed over to the door, ready to greet her adoring public.

A smile bloomed unbidden onto her face as Cameron pulled open the door.

"Good afternoon," the man with matinee idol looks on the other side of the door said, in what sounded like a posh English accent. To be honest, though, all English accents sounded pretty posh to Cameron. And Australian accents, for that matter. Canadian, too. It probably had to do with the fact they all sounded so exotic and cultured. Like the kind of accents which only existed in the TV.

The man wore a well-tailored seersucker suit across his lean, six foot frame, his hair combed in that messy "I hope it doesn't look like I actually spent all day combing this" way.

"I should probably introduce myself," the man added, as Cameron continued to smile at him, wondering if he was famous. "The name's Phillip Molloy. I work for the, uh, the local newspaper. Might I speak with the man of the house, Miss...?"

"Oh." Her smile turned upside down. "I'm Cameron Bailor. I just started working here..."

It was the nosy reporter guy, not someone famous who would sweep her off her feet and take her away from all this luxury.

"I see." He stared deep into her eyes, his expression looking all smoldering and brooding. "How much do you know about your employer, Ms. Bailor?"

"I'm terribly sorry," she said, needing to end this conversation before she swooned again, "but I have strict orders not to allow you to nose around the premises. I hope you understand. I really need this job, you see, so if you could--don't take this the wrong way, or anything--but if you could, you know, get lost, that would be a really big help to me. I'd really appreciate it."

"I don't think I can do that, Miss. You may not know it, but you're in grave danger. The man you work for is not what you think he is."

"You mean he's not a former star turned recluse who may have psychopathic tendencies?"

"Well, he's not *only* what you think he is," Molloy clarified. "He's...a vampire."

Her eyebrows tilted toward the ceiling. Cameron knew Mr. Gannen was eccentric and creepy, but she wasn't ready to believe that vampires actually existed. "Come again?"

"A vampire, Miss Bailor. He sleeps during the day. He kills at night by luring women into his home. He has no reflection. He can't stand the smell of garlic. He hates the color green-"

"I know what a vampire is," she explained, interrupting. "Like Wesley Snipes, right?"

"Precisely. But unlike Wesley Snipes, these vampires don't help people. They're

dangerous. You have to help me stop him. Despite my statement to the contrary, I'm not actually a reporter, working for your local newspaper. I am in fact something quite different. I make the world safer by disposing of dangerous creatures like Mr. Gannen."

She thought back to Tammy's phone in the garbage. Pauline's phone upstairs. Those phones hadn't been lost, after all, had they? They'd been cast aside after their owners had been drained of all precious fluids. That was the only answer, wasn't it?

Haberson's really gross neck wound. The red wine stains. The alibi. The creepy voice. The doilies. It all added up.

Cameron's boss actually was a vampire.

Even with a monstrous paycheck, could she in good conscience work for such a monster? Could she take his blood money and buy a nice apartment and a ton of awesome shoes?

Probably. Yeah. That sounded exactly like something she'd do.

"You're going to have to leave, Phillip," she reluctantly instructed the dreamy man with the TV accent. "I really need this job. If you don't leave, I'm afraid I'll have to call the cops."

Cameron felt terrible turning away such a hunk, but she tempered her distaste with thoughts of all the shoes she was going to buy in the upcoming years.

Phillip held up a hand. "Ms. Bailor, I have a proposition to offer you. Hear me out. I've been looking for a personal assistant for some time now. You're obviously qualified enough to work for a powerful man like Gannen, so you must be qualified enough to work for a bloke like me. Perhaps you'd rather fight on the side of good, instead of on the side of an evil, blood-sucking devil who will inevitably turn on you?"

"Hold on a minute," Cameron said, casting a suspicious eye toward him. "What's it pay?"

"Whatever you can carry out of every vampire's home. It can be quite lucrative, considering the wealth the undead tend to accumulate."

Ooh. Free stuff? From the homes of morally bankrupt individuals who had been gathering valuables from their victims for countless centuries?

Cameron brightened. "You've got yourself a deal, Mr. Molloy."

She stepped away from the door to permit the unfairly handsome vampire hunter access to Mr. Gannen's home.

"I look forward to working with you, then, Ms. Bailor," Molloy said, melting Cameron with his smile as he clasped her hand in his.

"Likewise," she breathed, finding it difficult to speak, melted as she was.

"Just give me a few minutes." He brushed past her. "And we'll be on our way."

Cameron watched him sweep through the mansion, adjusting his hair with his fingertips before drawing a wooden stake and its accompanying mallet from his coat.

"Oh, well," she said to herself, watching Molloy trot up the stairs to do away with her current boss. "It was fun while it lasted. Hopefully, I'll be a bit luckier with my next job. Vampire hunting can't be all that difficult, can it?"

***

Meet the Authors

Michael G. Williams – DADDY USED TO DRINK TOO MUCH

Michael G. Williams is a native of the Appalachian Mountains and grew up near Asheville, North Carolina. He describes his writing as wry horror or suburban fantasy: stories told from the perspectives of vampires, unconventional investigators, magicians and hackers who live in the places so many of us also call home. Michael is also an avid athlete, a gamer and a brother in St. Anthony Hall and Mu Beta Psi.

Patrick C. Greene - NIGHTBOUND

Some dark serendipity plopped a young Patrick Greene in front of a series of ever stranger films-and experiences-in his formative years, leading to a unique viewpoint. His odd interests have led to pursuits in film acting, paranormal investigation, martial arts, quantum physics, bizarre folklore and eastern philosophy. These elements flavor his screenplays and fiction works, often leading to strange and unexpected detours designed to keep viewers and readers on their toes.

Literary influences range from Poe to Clive Barker to John Keel to a certain best-selling Bangorian. Suspense, irony, and outrageously surreal circumstances test the characters who populate his work, taking them and the reader on a grandly bizarre journey into the furthest realms of darkness. The uneasy notion that reality itself is not only relative but indeed elastic- is the hallmark of Greene's writing.

Living in the rural periphery of Asheville North Carolina with his wife, youngest son and an ever-growing army of cats, Greene still trains in martial arts when he's not giving birth to demons via his pen and keyboard.

Visit his website: PatrickCGreene.com

In addition to his novel PROGENY, and the short story collection DARK DESTINIES, Greene has several film projects in the works, and just finished writing his second novel - THE CRIMSON CALLING -the first in the action-adventure vampire trilogy, The Sanguinarian Council.

Domyelle Rhyse - PROMISES

Domyelle Rhyse, or domy (as she prefers to be called), started writing at the age of 10 and fell in love with fantasy when a fifth grade teacher read The Hobbit to the class. She started annoying friends with weird stories in high school but didn't take her writing seriously until after earning a college degree in English and having a family that took pride in interrupting her every minute. Her short stories and articles have appeared in several online and print magazines and anthologies, including Aoife's Kiss, Beyond Centauri, Golden Visions, and Distant Passages: The Best from Double-Edged Publishing Vol. 1. As an editor and an admin of Dreaming In Ink Writers Workshop, she's had the honor of working with a number of authors whose works have been published by both small press and trade publishers. Denyse is the mother of four children and lives in Georgia with her chef husband, her autistic son, and three cats.

Billie Sue Mosiman – YE WHO ENTER HERE BE DAMNED

Author of more than 50 books, Billie Sue Mosiman is a thriller, suspense, and horror novelist, a short fiction writer, and a lover of words. In a diary when she was thirteen years old she wrote, "I want to grow up to be a writer." It seems that was always her course.

Her books have been published since 1984 and two of them received an Edgar Award Nomination for best novel and a Bram Stoker Award Nomination for most superior novel. Billie Sue has been a regular contributor to a myriad of anthologies and magazines, with more than 150 short stories published.

Chantal Noordeloos – THE BLOOD RUNS STRONG

Chantal Noordeloos (born in the Hague, and not found in a cabbage as some people may suggest) lives in the Netherlands, where she spends her time with her wacky, supportive husband, and outrageously cunning daughter, who is growing up to be a supervillain. When she is not busy exploring interesting new realities, or arguing with characters (aka writing), she likes to dabble in drawing.

In 1999 she graduated from the Norwich School of Art and Design, where she focused mostly on creative writing.

There are many genres that Chantal likes to explore in her writing. Currently Sci-fi Steampunk is one of her favourites, but her 'go to' genre will always be horror. "It helps being scared of everything; that gives me plenty of inspiration," she says.

Chantal likes to write for all ages, and storytelling is the element of writing that she enjoys most. "Writing should be an escape from everyday life, and I like to provide people with new places to escape to, and new people to meet."

Sarah I. Sellers – BLOOD TIES

When she's not saving the lives of moles and other small creatures, or playing with her incredibly cute suger-glider, Sarah Sellers is writing and drawing. From competing in her father's impromptu drawing contests as a small child, to writing her first short stories at the young age of 10, Sarah has always been intrigued and inspired by the arts.

Her literary influences range from the works of S. E. Hinton and Daniel Keyes, to the more contemporary fantasy of Maggie Stiefvater and Brenna Yovanoff.

Her first published work will be the short story Blood Ties featured in the Wrapped In Red vampire anthology published by Sekhmet Press LLC.

Justine Dimabayao – BORN OF THE EARTH

Born April 16, 1988, Justine Dimabayao came into the world with a flair for the arts. An introverted bibliophile who grew up in an Air Base in the Philippines and was educated in a Catholic school, Justine was exposed to a wide array of reading materials. It was not until she saw Bram Stoker's Dracula when she was 7 years old and read the movie's source material when she was 13 that she became fond of vampires and the mythology surrounding them. Inspired by Stephen King and J.K. Rowling, Justine aspires to be a novelist.

Brian D. Mazur – SHATTERING GLASS

In the summer of 2009, Brian's short story "Raven and the Darkness" appeared in Horror Bound's anthology Return of the Raven. 2011 saw "What She Dreams" in another Horror Bound publication, Fear of the Dark. In 2012 his short story, "Home Coming", was published in Wicked East Press', Behind Locked Doors and from Jaletta Celgg & Frances Pauli, the weedy anthology Wandering Weeds: Tale of Rabid Vegetation, is his horror/dark fantasy influenced, "Oh, Dark Tumbleweed". The last twenty years have seen numerous publications in smaller press magazines as well.

Brian also leads a local writing group of no specific genre, from which evolved his first public reading, June 2013.

Mark Parker – THE SCARLET GALLION

Mark Parker was born in the Midwest, but has lived all over the country, partly while serving in the United States Navy. For much of his life, he has called coastal New England home—a place rich in literary history—with authors such as Melville, Lovecraft, Poe, Hawthorne, and King, to influence his own mixed brand of horror, suspense, and mystery fiction.

He currently has three published works to his credit—*Way of the Witch (Book I of the Witch Saga)*; *Biology of Blood (Part I of the Southridge Vampires Series)*; and *Lucky You*, a standalone psychosexual thriller short—all available at Amazon.com. He is working on multiple projects: THE SCRIMSHAW

MURDERS, the first book in an historical whaling mystery series; HEADLINES, DEADLINES, the first in a series of cozy mysteries set in the fictional coastal town of Placid Point, Massachusetts, and his first full-length suspense novel, PERFECT DARKNESS, set against the scandal-plagued backdrop of the Roman Catholic Church, of which he has intimate knowledge having spent six years studying for the Roman Catholic priesthood. He holds a Bachelor of Arts degree in Philosophy, and is working towards his Master's Degree in Theology. He currently resides in Boston, MA, where he works in mental health and hospital education. Some of his hobbies include: travel, culinary arts, and all genres of fiction, when his writing schedule permits.

Maynard Blackoak – DANGEROUS DAN TUCKER

Maynard Blackoak is a freelance writer living in the backwoods of Pawnee County, Oklahoma. He began writing as a student in high school. His first piece was published in 1976 as part of an anthology of stories and poetry written by high school students in Oklahoma. He has written many short stories, reviews, articles and conducted interviews for various magazines. His latest work, Under the Black Oak Tree, a short story included in The Endlands Vol 2 anthology through Hobbes End Publishing, is currently available in print and ebook form.

Suzi M – BLOOD IN THE WATER

Lurking in a Pennsylvania town near historic Gettysburg, Suzi M is weaving webs of horror: including gothic, noir, ghosts, demons, angels, occult, and the occasional historic and/or post-apocalyptic thriller. Her storytelling has been compared to that of Tanith Lee and HP Lovecraft. Suzi's writing explores the thrill and the secrecy; the untold mysteries waiting in the shadows. In addition to a few other humans, including the tiny Hypnospawn, Suzi shares her home with a 30lb black house panther named Mr. Pants. When she's not busy with her own work or getting pictures and autographs with people who recognize her on the street, Suzi helps support the efforts of independent artists, writers, musicians, and film-makers. She is also a self-described "fiberfreak," finding time to spin, knit, crochet or weave when the muse allows. She will most likely achieve fame and fortune with her hand-crafted socks.

The Immortal War Series – comprised of NEMESIS, LAMIA, and THE TOWER – can be found in both print and Kindle formats.

In 2010, ten of Suzi's short stories were published in the international Cover Stories Euphictional Anthology.

Currently, Suzi is working on a several new projects and recently released Apocrypha of the Apocalypse, as well as The Murdered Metatron under the pseudonym James Glass and The Lazarus Stone (Conspiracy Edit) under the pseudonym Xircon.

Bryan W. Alaspa – VERMILION

Bryan W. Alaspa is a Chicago native and published author of over 20 works of fiction and non-fiction. He has written books in the genres of horror, thrillers, suspense, true crime, history, mysteries, young adult, paranormal and even romance.

When he's not writing, Bryan enjoys spending time with his beautiful wife, Melanie, and their two fur babies, Gracie and Pippa.

Michael David Matula – MY BOSS IS A VAMPIRE

Michael Matula is a novelist and story writer from Chicago, IL. He was born on a Friday the 13th, which could explain some of the darker themes in his writing. He once dreamed of becoming a comic artist, sketching pictures and caption bubbles in class when he really should have been studying. Unable to draw fast enough to keep up with all the words and images tumbling in his head, he started writing stories based on his characters instead. He ended up falling in love with writing and never really looked back.

His first novel, Try Not To Burn, is a paranormal thriller about three strangers who try to escape from the afterlife. It was released in late 2012 by Post Mortem Press, an indie publisher out of Cincinnati, Ohio.

Michael is currently working on the sequel to Try Not To Burn, and has a few other projects in the works.

You can follow all of our authors on Twitter -
#13Vampires

Keep up with the latest at
www.sekhmetpress.com

CPSIA information can be obtained at www.ICGtesting.com
Printed in the USA
LVOW13s2129140314

377453LV00001B/216/P

9 781491 026342